# Bad Blood

USA TODAY BESTSELLING AUTHOR
## SHYLA COLT

# Playlist

Deftones: Change
White Zombie: More Human Than Human
Rob Zombie: Dragula
Danzig: Mother
Rob Zombie: Living Dead Girl
Marilyn Manson: The Beautiful People
Shawn Mendes: In My Blood
Nirvana: You Know You're Right
Johnny Cash: Hurt
Imagine Dragons: Whatever It Takes
TWENTY ØNE PILØTS: Lane Boy
TWENTY ØNE PILØTS: Heathens
My Chemical Romance: Famous Last Words
TWENTY ØNE PILØTS: Ride
Boy Epic: Fifty Shades

# Dedication

*To everyone who supported me, and encouraged me to chase my dreams.*

Bad blood: a feeling of intense hatred or hostility; enmity

# Chapter One

### KEETA

NAKEETA ALVA WALKED THROUGH SOULSTONE burning a bundle of dried sage and envisioning white light flooding every inch of the building. Different energies traversed the metaphysical store all day. Some who came to her for advice and assistance carried negative energy along with them. From attachments to damaged auras, the building constantly housed diverse and at times conflicting energies.

She ended every day with a cleansing. Following her instinct, she zeroed in on a disturbance that upset her stomach. Blowing the smoke toward the books that lined the shelves, she moved closer to the front door. The incense burning in the holders helped fill every nook and cranny with the cleansing smoke. An inky black wisp of smoke rose up from the ground. She froze.

Her fingers clenched. The dark energy was alluring. It called to her, tempting her with its potency. She gritted her teeth. "Return from whence you came." Blowing the smoke directly onto the tendril, she imagined a blazing white-hot fire, eviscerating it like a laser. The energy shattered and drifted away. She bowed her head, breathing hard. Today, she won. Rattled, she quickly finished cleansing and moved to the room in the back. *It's time.*

Nakeeta focused on the deck of cards she held in her hand. She didn't read for herself often, but the unshakeable sense of dread had become a constant companion. Each day, she walked further out onto the razor's edge, certain she would run into one of the mishaps her mind conjured up constantly. Paranoid and anxious, the on-going experience left her frayed.

As a spiritual advisor, she understood how much the small things matter. Hunches, dreams, and gut feelings weren't to be ignored. Descended from a powerful medicine man, and a potent Voodoo priestess from 'Nawlins, spirits and the *other side* were ingrained in her from the minute she was born. Taught to embrace the unknown, along with her unusual talents, she found owning her own metaphysical store the only logical career choice. It allowed her to use her gift to help others.

Inhaling, she let her mind go blank as she shuffled the Oracle Cards. Today was about receiving messages. *Now I just need to get out of my own way and accept.* She was too close to the issue. It made an accurate Tarot reading impossible. Oracle cards were different. This was akin to going to a trusted friend for advice.

She laid out her first card. A flip of the glossy rectangle revealed a maiden with white hair, violet eyes, and brown skin beside a white unicorn. *Discernment.* Not all was what it seemed to be in her world. The message was clear. Her need for caution was not an imagined one. Card number two was a beautifully drawn blush pink unicorn hidden among the petals of a flower nearly the same shade of light pink.

A misty pastel background lent to the ethereal vibrations she felt exuding from the paper. *Rebirth.* Major change was coming. In order to be reborn, one had to experience a death of sorts. The third card representing her past made her balk. The black unicorn lined in a fiery silhouette was proud and majestic.

It exuded a masculine presence. *Anger.* No matter how she tried to leave her mistakes in the past, they continued to surface in the present. Regret was a slow working poison she needed to flush from her system.

Flying high on her success in life, she dabbled in the darkness, confident she could handle the black magic. The events that followed had done damage to her psyche and her aura, which took a year to fully heal from, and even more to forgive herself for. Her stomach bubbled like a cauldron. The days and nights that followed that event rushed back. Tiny bumps rose on her flesh, and her hairs stood on end.

Praying there would be a change of tide, she flipped the fourth card to see what her future held. *Receive.* A brown-skinned woman with curved ears and amber eyes leaned against a white unicorn and held a crystal ball. It couldn't be clearer. This represented her. *Open to what?* Inhaling, she forced her body to calm with rhythmic breathing.

Brow furrowed, she flipped the fifth card to reveal a unicorn reared back on its hind legs on top of a mountain. Sunlight beamed down through a murky sky, turning its horn into a beacon of light. Be open to the unknown, and leap without looking. It went against everything she practiced since she paid the price for her carelessness.

She flipped the next card and gasped. Two gray unicorns stood together. The male stood a head taller than the female. His stance was protective, and his soft brown gaze was full of tenderness for his mate. Butterflies floated around them. *Mate.* Someone would be entering her life to help her understand what was to come. Unlike before she would listen to the words of wisdom the card held.

She shuffled the cards with jerky, agitated motions. For comfort, she ran over the people and events occurring in her life. Instead of putting her at ease, the reading amped up her anxiety. Her concentration had been riddled full of 'what if' shotgun shells. There would be no figuring this out tonight. Growling, she released a puff of air, blowing the riotous black curls off her forehead.

She arranged the cards into a compact square, placed them facedown on her length of black silk, and wrapped them. Satisfied with her bundling, she returned them to the black velvet pouch where they lived, and pushed away from the table.

Stretching her arms above her head, she rose onto her tiptoes, releasing the tension that had built in her spine. Her gaze danced around SoulStone. The tranquil Caribbean-blue walls and beloved knickknacks she'd collected over the years never failed to anchor her to the here and now.

She fought hard for this place. Working two, sometimes three jobs to pay her bills and save up while she did readings for family, friends, and eventually clients on the side. The day she turned in her resignations, five years prior, had been a giant milestone.

A boom of thunder sounded in the distance, jerking her from her musing. She looked out the window. The blue sky had turned gray, and plump clouds tinged a menacing dark hue blotted out the sun. A storm was rolling in fast, carrying a sinister vibe with it. The wind whistled outside, rattling the shutters on her windows. Urgency struck, setting off internal alarms. Her skin tingled and her mouth dried. Grabbing her black purse off the desk, she ran from the door to escape an invisible foe.

Fat, angry drops of rain splattered against the shop windows. Her hand shook as she twisted the key in the tumbler. As she stumbled away from the door, her ears strained to detect a threat. Cold water slipped down into the hollow between her breasts, and across her bare back. Shivering, she stepped into the light drizzle.

Her heels tapped a manic tune on the concrete as she strode down the sidewalk, clutching the handle of her purse. A chill that had nothing to do with the rain hit her body and penetrated down to the bone. She risked a quick glance over her shoulder. *Nothing.*

Her stride became a light jog. Ignoring the protest the soles of her feet made as they took the impact from three inches in the air, she made the fifteen-minute walk in about seven minutes. Her chest heaved with the exertion as she stopped at the crosswalk across her street. A vivid bolt of lightning streaked across the sky, and the heavens opened.

She placed the clutch over her head to keep the shard-like droplets off her face as best as she could. Cars zipped by, throwing water onto her open toe-shoes. *Squish.* Wrinkling her nose, she willed the light to change. When the stoplight went from green to yellow, she mentally cheered.

All she wanted to do was get into her house. A few more feet and she could shut out the world for the rest of the evening. Screeching tires made her jump back from the curb. She lifted her head just in time to see two blinding circles of light.

�֎·֍

THICK FOG PAINTED THE WORLD around her white. She wrapped her arms around her waist, disoriented and frightened. Unable to see more than an inch in front of her face, she stood paralyzed. Rustling in the distance set her heart racing. *There's something out there.* A throaty growl followed by a long howl set her feet into motion. Lunging to the left, she took off full tilt.

A marsh-like ground gave beneath her bare feet. The scent of smoke and leather drifted up from the tan hide dress she wore. The material flapped against her skin. She stumbled. Her arms flailed as she struggled to regain her balance. Breathing heavily, she stared at the unyielding white, seeking clues.

The howls continued. They grew closer and more intense as more wolves joined in. Gooseflesh broke out over her flesh. The sound surrounded her as they circled her, boxing her in. She struggled to breathe as her chest tightened and her heart raced.

A large animal broke through the fog. She screamed, throwing her hands up to protect her face. The impact never came as the large, gray wolf with amber eyes landed beside her. She lowered her arms and watched as it grew to a two-legged man with dark black hair and dark eyes. His olive skin stood out against his breechcloth and leggings. A dark gray wolf pelt hung around his shoulders. She took a step back.

There was something evil in the depths of his obsidian eyes. *Skin Walker.* He held out his palm.

*Ancestors, protect me.* This was old magic.

"You are of my line." His heavily accented English gave her pause.

"What?"

"You are my descendant. I will not hurt my own blood."

"Where am I?"

"You are in the dreaming place. Not awake, yet not asleep. I have brought you here."

"Why?"

"To show you where it all went wrong."

Narrowing her gaze, she shook her head. "Where what went wrong?"

"Wait."

The fog swirled into a series of tornadoes dancing around her like giant sentinels. She closed her eyes against the dizzying effect.

"Look."

She opened her eyes in response to the guttural command.

They stood at the entrance of a cave. The moonlight shone down, illuminating the arch. A fire crackled in the center spilling its warm glow on the grizzly scene in front of her. The man sat in front of large stones fixed around the fire. A red lump rested on each stone. His mouth was covered with blood along with his hands. He grabbed one of the … hearts? Then, he took a large bite.

Her stomach roiled.

"I wanted more power than I should have had. Each animal has a spirit. When you ingest their heart still warm and coursing with their life, you take them into yourself. This is bad magic. I was warned. I ignored them because I did not understand what it would cause."

He moved on to a dark purple lump.

'What is that?"

"The beginning of the end of the work our line once did to save humanity."

He lifted the organ to his mouth and sank his teeth in deep. Dark blood oozed down onto his hand. "It's my first sampling of blood from a beast. One who walks only at night and lives on the life force of others."

"A vampire?" she whispered.

"Yes."

Choking, he dropped the heart with a wet plop. His body twitched. He foamed at the mouth and fell onto the ground in what looked like a seizure.

"This was the start of my transformation and the weakening of the spell we cast to keep man and beasts separated. I did not stop here. I consumed the ones who walk as wolves under the moon and one of our own. A powerful medicine man."

"You consumed human flesh," she whispered, horrified.

"It is up to you to fix what I have done now."

"What—"

He placed a hand on her shoulder, and pain flowed through her body. She cried out, arching as violent energy moved through her.

## CREWE

The shush of the ventilator interrupted the silence in the room as it moved up and down, breathing for the woman who lay lifeless in the hospital bed. Her heart-shaped face was a canvas of blues and purples. They'd shorn her curls and shaved her hair down to operate, and then stapled her skull back together like Humpty Dumpty. The short buzz made her features sharper beneath the swollen flesh.

He tried to envision her before the accident, healthy and whole. She was an echo of her mother with a few of her father's features thrown in. Beulah and Arve Alva had come to him seeking help for their daughter. Powerful, poised, and distraught, the couple had admitted to hiding their daughter away.

*Nakeeta.* He rolled the name around in his head. She was nearly lost to them. The van did a real number on her. It was touch and go. For a moment, he thought they were too late, and the one chance they had for a fresh start was gone. It took years to trace the correct bloodlines, and longer still to narrow down the cities. His people had no luck finding her until today when they were contacted.

He shuddered thinking of the failed attempts with the wrong people. The horrific results would stay with him for the rest of his undead life. The blood turned them into slaves—or worse, it burned through their body, ravaging them like an infectious disease.

Reaching inside his black trench coat, he removed a bag of blood so dark it looked black. Walking to her bedside, he swapped it with the O positive currently flowing through her veins. Regret sucker punched him in the gut as his blood traveled down the I.V. and into her system. Had he delivered a death sentence or discovered their salvation?

Either way, life would never be the same for her. She had bad blood in her now. It made him feel guilty. He never wanted this life, and yet he'd passed it on—the one thing he'd promised himself he'd never do. They were both victims to the wheel of fate. Once it spun, you learned to rotate with it or be crushed by its unstoppable force. Crewe held his breath and watched as the bruises began to fade slowly.

It wouldn't be long before her body healed itself. Sitting in the navy-blue hospital seat beside her bed, he closed his eyes and waited for the transfusion to complete. They'd know soon enough if they got it right. He was tired. They all were. For years, they fought a losing battle as the spells that kept them in check waned.

More and more Vampires walked in the day. Coupled with the madness ravaging them like a plague as the press of years weighed down on increasingly fragile minds, the situation had spiraled out of control. The blood of his friends stained his hands scarlet. Their ghosts haunted him, seeking justice.

The council could barely keep up with the cover-ups. He'd heard whispers of the Weres growing in numbers too large to be supported on their land. Time was running out. Once she woke, he needed to get her on the fast track to becoming their savior or prepared for the beginning of the end. Rubbing his temple with his thumb and middle finger, he did his best to relax. He needed to be ready for the insanity waiting to devour them whole.

# Chapter Two

### Keeta

Nakeeta's eyelids fluttered open. Sunlight pierced her retinas. She automatically clamped her lids shut in response. Opening her mouth to cry out, she choked on something lodged in her throat. Gagging, she tugged at the length of flexible tubing, and thrashed in the bed. High-pitched tones squealed, stabbing her eardrums like sharp knives.

"Ms. Alva, please stop! If you pull your tubes out, you could do some serious danger."

A hand clamped down on her wrist like steel.

"You're in the hospital. You were hit by a van, and you've been in a medically-induced coma for the past couple of days. We placed the breathing tubes in because your brain was too swollen to gauge the damage." Their words penetrated through the haze of confusion and she stilled. Memories rushed back. The blinding light followed by a pain unlike any she had ever experienced. It felt as if her bones splintered from the inside out and collapsed on themselves.

"Good, we're going to let you go now. I know the tubes are uncomfortable, but we have to be careful not to remove them too soon. We're calling your doctor now, but we'd like to check your stats before he gets here. My name is Andrea, and I'm your daytime nurse." Nakeeta forced her eyes to open a sliver. The woman beside her had flame red hair, tucked behind her ear.

Her gaze blurred and wavered too much to focus on her features. However, the warmth and compassion that radiated from the nurse's petite frame needed no explanation.

"You're with me now?" Andrea asked.

Nakeeta nodded.

"Wonderful."

Andrea explained every action before she did it, with firm, yet gentle hands.

"I can't understand what I'm seeing. You've done weeks, maybe months of healing in a matter of days." The awe in her voice tugged at memory in the far corners of her brain. She chased it, but the elusive butterfly escaped the net. "How do you feel about trying to sit up?"

Nakeeta managed what she hoped was an agreeable grunt. The whir of the bed and the slow propulsion forward made her heart jump in her chest like a frog. She opened her eyes again, more slowly. The watered-down ache was bearable. Her vision came back into focus, and Andrea smiled.

"Welcome back, sweetheart."

She wanted to smile. The door swung open. An older man with salt-and-pepper hair cropped short, a round face, and square, black-rimmed glasses stepped inside of the room.

"You are quite an extraordinaire, Ms. Alva. I'm amazed by your progress." He walked over toward the bed, his white coat flying out behind him to reveal a pair of powder blue scrubs.

"I'm Dr. Phillips. Your body and brain have been through a lot of trauma. I'm going to check your vitals. Nurse Andrea, her chart, please." He took the clipboard into his hand and scanned the papers.

"I recommend we leave the tube in for a few more hours." He smiled. "I know you really want to get it out, but it's better to be safe than be sorry." He pulled a penlight out of his pocket. "Now let me get a glimpse into those pretty, green eyes."

Whimpering she fluttered her lids, staving off the moisture that pooled in her eyeballs.

"Good, they respond to light as they should. I'll take your pulse." He placed his fingers on the pulse point in her wrist with a cold hand and long, elegant fingers. "Perfect. I'm going to finish my vitals check, and then I think we may be able to move you out of ICU to critical condition. That way you can have visitors. Your family has been camped out in the waiting rooms since they arrived not too long after you were admitted." He righted to a standing position and began to inspect the machines, making notations and nodding.

"Is the pain medication sufficient? Blink once for yes, and twice for no." He glanced up, and she blinked once.

"My dear, considering what you've been through, you are a modern miracle. One I am pleased to be able to witness. You're on the fast track to getting out of here within a month."

*I must've been road kill when they brought me here the way everyone's acting like I'm Lazarus risen.*

"Now I'm going to update your family on everything that's happened. Andrea will be checking on you regularly, but if you should need something a call button is located on your left, right beside the buttons that lower and raise your bed." He walked over to a tiny blue box with bright stripes of color. "I'm going to administer another dose of morphine. It'll make you sleep. Right now, that's the best thing for you. If all goes well, the tubes will be removed when you wake up. Then we can talk relocation." He pressed a button, and she rested her head against the pillow. *Maybe I'll wake up, and this will all be a horrible nightmare.* Even as she drifted off, she recognized the thought for the lie it was.

HUMMING PULLED HER FROM THE void.

"Mama?" she croaked as she peeled open her eyes in response to the gentle voice and the light squeeze to her hand.

"My sweet child. That's it. Let me see those pretty eyes, bug."

The light was kinder to her retinas as she focused on the gently lined, oval-shaped face that was dear to her.

"Praise God," her mother whispered. She stood and bent down, kissing her forehead. Her coarse curls tickled her face. Her nose twitched in response. Her mother smoothed her hair back from her face and sank back into her seat. Nakeeta smacked her lips.

"Let me get you some water." Her mother hurried off as she acclimated herself with the waking world. *How long have I been here?* Her mother returned with a large, pink plastic cup with a straw. "Let's get you sitting up." Her mother hit the button and slowly pushed her up into an upright position.

"Better?"

"Yes," she rasped.

"Here you are." She held the cup out, and she wrapped her lips around a straw and sucked the cool water down her sore throat. The relief drew a hum from her throat. Pulling away, Keeta cleared her throat.

"I'm so sorry. Times run out," her mother whispered.

"What are you talking about, Mom?" She furrowed her brow.

"We did our best to protect you, Keeta. Growing up we tried to keep you away from all things magical, but the power ran too deep. The spirits tried to tell me, but I was too stubborn to listen. You were my child, and I wanted the best for you. Your magic was a part of you that refused to be ignored or denied. So, we switched gears, tried to prepare you for what we knew would come, and hid you for as long as we could. I knew the moment I saw you and looked into your eyes you were the one our family had prophesied about."

"Hid me from what?" *Is this some sort of fever dream? Am I still in a comma?*

"Everyone who would use you as a weapon." Her mother's whisper was full of sorrow and desperation.

"Use me? Mom, you're not making any sense." Exasperated, she huffed. Her body ached, and her head felt barely attached to her shoulders. A combination of the powerful medication and exhaustion that came from healing warped her perception. A hazy recollection of a dream tugged at her. *What was I supposed to remember?* Her brain protested the strain with a dull throbbing at her temples that stopped her from thinking too hard.

Her mother held her hand. "You're different."

"Yes, like our entire family is," Keeta replied, unsure of what her mother wished to convey. She'd never been the type to beat around the bush before. Why hesitate now?

"Yes, but you have power. A scary amount of it. *Things* have always been drawn to you. Even with us cloaking you to dampen your light, it shone so brightly." She closed her eyes and shook her head. "We tried to do right by you, Keeta. Now I'm not sure we were right."

"Mom, you're scaring me." Her voice warbled.

"Destiny will only be denied so long, baby. Yours is at hand."

Her stomach knotted. The storm that had been threatening overhead was finally breaking.

"Our family is made up of more than powerful magic workers. We descend from a long lineage of gifted magical beings. It goes back further than you can imagine, and some of the spells created and cast changed the shape of the world as we know it." She glanced around nervously. "I'm not sure how much time we have. You're a part of a bigger plan, Keeta. The laws keeping humans safe are crumbling into themselves. You can help change that. I won't tell you it'll be easy, or comfortable, but it's necessary. If I could take this burden from you, I would." She shook her head. "But it wasn't meant for me."

"I don't understand. *What* am I supposed to do? Why?" Keeta shook her head. She'd never seen her mother this distraught. Dark circles ringed her puffy red eyes. Regret and apprehension stiffened her muscles and turned her dark brown eyes nearly black.

"I want to tell you more." Her mother bowed her head. Her mouth clamped shut as if it'd been glued together. "Mmm. Mmmm." She struggled to speak. Her face turned purple.

"Mom?" She gripped the blankets hard and leaned forward. "Breathe!"

Her mother gasped, greedily sucking in air as her slender form trembled. Tears rolled down her face in a steady stream of salty water. "I can't. God help me, I can't." Her anguished cries sliced at Keeta's heart.

"You can't what?" she whimpered, feeling her mother's pain as her own.

Exasperated, her mother threw her hands into the air and shook her head so hard she thought she might strain a muscle. "T-the d-deal," she stuttered, stumbling over her words

"What deal?" Her stomach plummeted, and her heartbeat spiked. The monitors beeped nosily in response.

"The one she made to save your life," a masculine voice answered from the doorway.

Her spine stiffened. The room felt too small. She shrank back against her pillow. His aura was dark and powerful. Nearly six-foot with pale blond hair, crystalline blue eyes, and cheekbones that could draw blood, he oozed strength and dominance.

*Predator.* He slammed against the wall, pinned into place. She gasped. *Did I do that?*

"Nakeeta!" her mother hissed.

She'd never been able to manifest her powers this way. She trembled. Images of the powerful medicine man and his words filled her brain. A headache burst through her head.

"Stop this," her mother demanded.

*I don't know how.* She wouldn't share that weakness in front of this—

His eyes flashed red.

*Vampire.*

His thin, pink lips curved, revealing fangs. "Now she realizes. Because you are vulnerable and your brain is muddled, I will allow your impertinence to slide this once."

"What have you done, Mama?" She struggled to undo the process and release him from her hold.

"Saved your life. Now do as the man asks."

"He's no man."

"All the more reason to listen to your mother," he purred.

She sensed the tightly leashed beast he held back. A lock clicked open inside of her, and she retracted her power.

"You've got a lot to learn," he drawled.

*Does he know?*

"And I suppose you'll be the one who'll teach me?" Sitting up straight in bed, she held her head high, ignoring the protests of stiff muscle. There'd never been any love lost between witches and vampires. She peered down her nose at the bloodthirsty, emotionally bereft savage who studied her from beneath lazily lowered lids. Common sense told her to back off. Their brutality was a thing of legend. The anger burning brightly blotted out her ability to rationalize.

"Nakeeta. He's the reason you're alive."

Images of her ancestor gorging himself on hearts flittered in her head. *When you ingest the life force of another being still warm and fresh, you take them into yourself.*

"No," she cried.

"Do you understand what that means? We are connected, and you are something more than you once were."

She fisted the sheets at her side. "What have you done to me?"

"We don't know," the vampire said honestly. For a moment, she thought she saw compassion in his artic blue gaze. "Vampirism has never been as cut and dry as the movies make it. Not everyone can be turned, and the effects vary. You won't be like me. I didn't drain you and give you enough blood to cause a transition, but there will be changes. Given your genetic make-up, and the way you responded with that powerful display, it's already begun."

"Why would you agree to this?" Keeta said, directing her question at the mysterious vampire. Her mother's reasoning was valid. His motives were unknown and sketchy at best.

"We are not enemies—" he began.

"Centuries of history say otherwise." She refused to give an inch.

"We want the same thing," he said.

Keeta's brow furrowed. "What's that?" she asked skeptically.

"Peace between our races."

"You need to listen to him, Keeta. What he has to say could make or break life as we know it."

*It's up to you to fix this now.* The words echoed in her head, confirming the truth. The bed began to rattle. Metal clanked as things feel to the floor.

"Keeta, you need to calm down." Her mother's panicked plea barely registered. A red haze of anger built up inside.

"Oh my god! Her eyes."

Iron bands clamped around her forearms.

"Look at me."

She fell headfirst into a crimson-colored gaze.

## CREWE

"Rest." He overloaded her senses, shutting her body down as he slipped through her mental shields with ease. Her body went limp.

"What have you done?"

"She is resting. We have to act now. This may get worse before she learns control." He ignored the bitter scent of apprehension and fear flooding her pores.

"Louis, Pierce. It's time to initiate stage two." He spoke to the men he had posted on the floor knowing they could hear him. *Time for cleanup.*

"What's happening?" Her mother moved closer.

He laid Keeta's body back against the bed. "They will alter memories and strike Keeta from the records. We don't want to be tracked or leave any reason for them to seek her out. This type of healing is unprecedented. The doctor would have already contacted others if we had not intervened."

"Her shop. Her life here—"

"Is over until further notice," he stated, cutting her off.

"She's poured all she had into that shop! If you destroy everything she's built what will that do to her? You saw how unbalanced she became."

He growled. Humans and their petty attachments to temporary things.

"There are far more important things at stake, witch."

"You may know how vampires think, but I know my daughter. Humans need a reason to keep fighting. When change sweeps in like a stormy sea, we need an anchor to hold us."

He paused to consider her words. "What do you need?"

"Money to pay the bills. I will call on family to keep the store going, but it will take time for them to travel here."

"Done." What was money to someone such as he? Money accumulated over time and he had more than a human could spend in a thousand lifetimes.

He caught the scent of Pierce outside before the door opened. White-blond fringe fell across his eyes. The style might be popular nowadays, but he ached to go at it with a pair of cutting scissors.

"Is it done?"

Pierce nodded. "I've taken care of the computer data, and Louis is using his special persuasion to erase the doctor's thoughts. Is it safe to move her so soon?"

"Believe me when I say she's ready. We've allowed her to heal for a week. Any longer and the questions will begin to pile up and leak outside of the hospital walls, becoming a larger containment issue."

"All right." Pierce held up his hands. "I was just playing devil's advocate. It's my job."

"Don't act like it doesn't get your rocks off." Crewe rolled his eyes. "Horse's ass. Send Andrea to me the moment she logs in for her next shift."

Chuckling, Pierce retreated from the room.

"It's so easy to manipulate us humans." The bitterness was heavy in her mother's voice.

"You know witches aren't so easily managed," Crewe replied as he watched Keeta's vitals. They weren't out of the woods. The power he felt from her was great. He'd seen others burn out from less.

"And where will you take her now?"

"Telling you defeats the purpose of secrecy."

"I am her mother—"

He lifted a perfectly manicured hand to cut her off. "You made the oath and sealed it with your blood. Don't get all holier than thou with me now."

"What other choice did I have?"

"The same you have now. None."

She dropped her head. He smelled the salty water of tears. The door opened, and the petite nurse with periwinkle-blue-colored eyes entered.

"Hello, Andrea, lovely to see you today." A mental push sent his power up to his eyes. "You never met Nakeeta Alva. You've spent the past few weeks tending the patients here and dealing with normal shifts. Nothing extraordinary has occurred. As a matter of fact, you've been bored."

"I've been bored. Same shift different day."

"That's my girl. Now you'll go do your rounds and avoid this room for the next hour."

"I must go attend to my other patients now."

"Enjoy your evening. I was never here."

"You were never here," she agreed before walking away.

He remained in the chair monitoring Keeta's vitals as his team wiped minds and camera feed. He visited her nightly after visiting hours; sat by her bed and slipped in her mind to see her dreams. She was vibrant color in motion.

A beautiful soul with untapped powers she did not realize existed.

*I won't let this break you, Keeta. That I can promise. Come hell or high water I will defend you with my last breath and keep that amazing mind of yours intact.* There'd be no more casualties on his watch. Using the bond they shared, he sent her into a deeper sleep.

"How will I know she's okay?" her mother asked quietly.

"We will send word." He rose. "Now, my lovely, we have to get you up and out of here." Perusing the machines, he quickly configured the best way to disconnect her. Unlike their portrayal on television, his people weren't blood-crazed maniacs completely guided by instinct. They were intelligent, capable, and everywhere. Moving around the room faster than the human eye could track, he disabled the machines, unhooking her. He lifted her into his arms, savoring the warmth that seeped into his bones.

It was one of the things he'd missed most about being alive—the ability to generate heat. She nuzzled her nose into his neck, and he flinched, unused to the contact. He exited the room.

Pierce let out a wolf whistle. "I couldn't tell she was a looker under all of the bruises."

Crewe hissed as his protective instincts rose. His fangs distended and he stared the startled man down.

Pierce lifted his hands, palms outward. "Hey! I didn't mean anything by it, boss."

The reaction scared him. This should not work like a normal sire bond. *Had her witchy powers intensified his feelings?* With so much on the line, he didn't have time to fumble around like a man in the dark looking for a light switch. He concentrated on the sweet smell of the woman clutched in his arms. The blood rage receded. His vision returned to normal, and the urge to rip out Pierce's throat calmed.

"New rules ... opinions about Ms. Alva are kept to yourselves."

"I'll spread it around." Pierce swallowed hard.

The stench of fear and aggression poured off Pierce in waves. It shamed Crewe—he prided himself on control. A disorderly vampire was a dangerous one. They held too much power to wield it irresponsibly. He found that out the hard way. Images of blood and severed limbs accompanied a phantom metallic taste in his mouth. That night in the town, he'd gorged himself on the blood of innocents—men, woman, and children. None were safe from his hunger. He would've been put down if it hadn't been for Dregan. He wouldn't let his adopted sire down now that he'd been assigned this colossal task.

Louis walked up with a crew of ten behind him.

"Are we ready to make our exit?"

"Yes, after we leave we'll finish erasing our exit from the van," Louis assured him.

"Good. I'm going to take her home and prepare her for travel. If anything comes up contact me immediately before I'm out of range." He used his speed to make his way to the SUV without appearing like he'd kidnapped an unconscious woman. After quickly buckling her into the car, he pulled away from the hospital. Time was against them. He needed to observe her changes, train her and gain her trust before the spell gave way completely. His spine tingled and his neck heated. *I'm being watched.* He casually checked his mirrors. Increasing his speed, he took a sharp left unexpectedly, sped up, then pulled down a side street and killed his headlights.

Studying the street, he waited for a car to pass. The sensation of being observed never left. Cracking the window, he tilted his head he sniffed the air. The scent of fur and woods made him cringe. *Wolves.* Snarling, he growled a warning as he moved back onto the road. It wasn't unusual for werewolves to make themselves known in their territory, but he couldn't take chances with his precious cargo. Not everyone wanted the spell to be salvaged. His nose told him there were at least six, enough to be a scouting party meant to send a warning.

Unwilling to lead them back to the temporary dwelling, he opened up the engine, weaving through traffic. If they wanted to catch him, they'd have to work for it. The street lamps burst. Darkness fell. The SUV jerked to the left and slammed into a parked a car. The passenger door groaned in protest as it caved. The roof dented in as two large bodies landed on it. Claws slashed at the roof. He slammed on his brakes. A yelp sounded as a body crashed into the car in front of him. Throwing the vehicle into reverse, he turned his head, driving backward on the sidewalk to avoid the cars. The two wolves on the roof clawed for purchase.

A claw punctured the roof. He slammed on his brakes, jerking the wheel to the left and right as he tried to shake them off. Spinning the car, he pinned Keeta's body down as he changed directions. Nails scratched across the pavement as he lost another one. Hitting reverse, he rolled over the prone body with a sickening crunch. The last wolf swung down. Crewe punched his fist through the window and grabbed the wolf's throat, and sinking his nails into his jugular he ripped his throat free. Hot blood splattered across his face. He thrust the corpse onto the ground and floored the gas.

Taking the back roads, he frequently scanned the streets, sniffing the air. Satisfied, he doubled back and double clicked the button on his steering wheel.

"Blue tooth audio. Call Dregan."

"You have her?" The smooth baritone came through the speakers.

"I do. The wolves just attacked us in the car."

"To protect their turf or to get to the girl?"

Crewe glanced at the woman muttering in her sleep. "I'm not sure. I didn't stop to ask them."

"What are you going to do?"

"I need the plane ready to go within the next hour. I need her in a secure location."

"She's survived the transfusion so swiftly?" Blood was a tricky thing.

"As far as I can tell. She's powerful. I had to command her to sleep in the hospital."

"Tell me," Dregan said.

He described the scene.

"If the madness takes hold in her we're all lost."

"I know." Crewe tightened his grip on the steering wheel

"Do whatever it takes to gain her trust and prepare her. We need her own our side."

"I understand."

"I know you do. We've lost too many already." Silence feel between them. "I'll make the call. The jet will be ready. Where will you take her?"

"The same place you taught me."

"You will keep me posted."

"Yes, sir."

They disconnected, and he wondered once more if he'd be able to pull this off.

# Chapter Three

### Keeta

As she swam up from the darkness, the feeling of pressure and a loud buzz filled her ear. She smacked her lips in an attempt to moisten her bone-dry mouth. Clearing her aching throat, she pried open her lids. She squinted, struggling to adjust her vision to the dim lighting. A blue light illuminated a curved ceiling. She became aware of her surroundings all at once. Jerking in her seat, she knocked the long, black duster off her body. *Why am I in a plane?*

"You're awake then."

She turned to look across the aisle at the man who had turned her entire life upside down. "You," she seethed.

"Saved your life from carnivorous wolves while you slumbered? Yes. You're welcome by the way."

"You've ruined me," she snarled, clutching the expensive wooden armrests to keep from slashing at his face with her nails.

"I kept you from destroying the hospital. A quick reminder, we're in the air now, and I won't hesitate to put you down again if you can't control yourself."

She gritted her teeth and inhaled, fighting the rage building in her gut. That was where things went pear-shaped the last time.

"What have you done?"

"I don't have the answers you seek. This is new territory for both of us."

"Where are you taking me?" She focused on each word. There was a part of herself she didn't recognize. A vengeful banshee hell-bent on destruction and revenge. Dark emotions clouded her brain, making it hard to think straight.

"What are you feeling right now?"

The question startled her. "What am I feeling?" The words were poison dripping from her tongue and spilling from her lips. "Do I look like a toy you can play with?"

"No. You look like a person who needs help. When I first woke as a vampire the only thing I knew was a sense of famine. That gnawing pit at the bottom of your stomach demanding to be filled is hunger."

"I'm not a vampire."

"No. So what is it you crave?"

"Power," she whispered. The anger was a side effect from denying herself. She wanted to hurt him and revel in the newly gained power. Her body shook. It was like trying to kick black magic all over again. *Make him hurt. Show him you aren't one to be trifled with,* the voices whispered in her ear, and the parts of her she loathed most rose up, eager to answer. It sat back on its hind legs, salivating as it awaited its next command. It was a disconcerting feeling being split in two. As if another being lived in her body.

"You must control the hunger." He gripped her forearms. "It can never be the other way around."

Observing him was like peering at him from a distance. There was safety in the backseat. It kept the fear and pain away. In a matter of days, she'd lost everything.

"The more you give in, the harder it becomes to regain control. Fight it, or you doom us all with your cowardice."

His words jolt her like a slap to the face. "I am no coward."

"Prove it."

"You know nothing about me, vampire." The arm of the chair snapped off in her hands. She tossed it aside and zeroed in on the man across from her. His head snapped back. She twisted her hand, tossing him into the aisle. The magic gave her a rush. He stood at a speed too fast for her to track. Slammed back into the wall of the airplane, she clawed at the hand wrapped around her throat, constricting her airway.

"Is that all you have, witch?"

Anger simmered inside of her, a pot ready to boil over. *Show him.* Ignoring the fact that he held her life in his hands, she focused on the finger wrapped around her throat. They turned bright red. He released her.

"Is this what you meant?" she asked huskily.

His eyes flickered red, and he bared his fangs. "Right now, all I see is a witch so focused on her own emotions she can't see the bigger picture. If you don't get a handle on the hunger, you'll watch the entire world burn down around you while it laughs at your anguish. I'm not here to play games while you figure it all out. If you attack me again, I will no longer hold back."

The words sucker punched her soul. Shaken from the trance, she slammed a lid on her lust for power.

He narrowed his gaze. "Nakeeta?"

"Y-yes," she whispered shakily. Appalled, she wrapped a hand around her throat. She cast her gaze down in shame. *How could I act like that?* She didn't recognize the person who inhabited the body she'd been born in.

"This is your companion now. The hunger is a rude symbiotic guest who constantly seeks to gain control."

"You feel this all the time?" she asked, horrified.

"Every second of every day," he replied solemnly.

The admission turned her preconceived notions about vampires upside down. How could they hold onto any semblance of sanity?

"How did you know that wasn't me?"

"Your eyes. Unlike mine, they turn purple." He sighed. "I don't know you, but I have a sense of the person you are. We don't have time to become friends. I'm your teacher. I will show you what you need to know. And if you're a fast learner, and smart enough to listen to me, you might survive what's to come."

She scowled at his highhanded words. "I don't even know your name."

"Crewe. I won't ask you to trust me, because that can only be earned with time and actions. For now, you have no choice but to allow me to be your guide."

Life without choice was a prison. The visions of the Native American warrior flashed in her mind. Centuries later, his poor decisions kept him from finding rest in the afterlife. She refused to repeat his mistakes. "Don't think because we're stuck together you can treat me any kind of way. Your kind has always thought they were above everyone else. I will be treated with respect, and in return, I'll treat you the same."

"So, the witch has a bite on her own."

"More than you can imagine," she promised.

His eyes widened, and she looked away, unable to hold his azure stare. They were connected by an invisible link. There was no time for fear or cowering, so she stared him down in defiance, swallowing down the fear. "What is this?" she questioned, gesturing between them.

"Our bond."

"What does it do?"

"That's ..." he paused, "still to be determined."

"Is that your way of admitting you don't know?" She wrapped her arms beneath her chest.

He studied her like an experiment that should be observed from behind a glass. "The changes aren't a formulaic equation that adds up to the same amount every time, and you are different."

Shifting in her seat, she picked at the oversized white T-shirt and sweatpants she wore in lieu of her hospital gown. She didn't dare think too hard on what he saw when he dressed her. "Are you planning on going into greater detail, or do you enjoy withholding information?"

"When we arrive."

"Our final destination. Another thing I'd like to know."

He cast an exasperated look her way. Clearly, this wasn't a man used to being questioned. "An isolated country estate in England."

"How long did you keep me under?"

"Long enough. We'll be arriving in the next hour."

"And then?" she goaded.

"We'll begin training."

She turned away from him and stared at the indent her body left in the metal. Stunned, she ran her hand down the back of her head checking for lumps or blood.

"You're heartier than a normal human now."

"Permanently?" she asked, unsure how she felt about the new mutant status.

"I can't say."

He eased out of her space and breathing became easier.

Her jaw dropped as a panel opened to allow the jet to fly into what appeared to be an underground manmade cavern. It closed with a final clank that set her on edge.

"We will head to the house now."

Rising, she followed him off the jet onto a landing pad. "What about the pilot?"

"He'll be leaving once we move into the underground tunnel that leads to the house."

"So, it's just … us?" The thought made her nervous.

"For now. It's best this way. No distractions. What do you know about your bloodline?"

"Not enough."

"Our people have never lived in harmony. But there used to be enough space for everyone. Before overdevelopment, overpopulation, and evasive technology. Vampires are a mix of genetics and magic. When man developed a higher consciousness, some turned toward the light, leaving the caves, and others … kept to the shadows. Man and magic have always walked hand in hand. Those in the light forgot while we remembered."

She paused in mid-step. "Wait. Are you telling me all vampires were once human?"

"Not all, but the first of us. We're not so different. We share a common ancestry. Had you turned right instead of left you could've been what we are."

"No." She shook her head, angered by his assumptions. "There must be more to this."

"The story says a man came into the caves offering us a better life, one where we could walk outside of our dwellings, even if only at night. He said it'd come at a price, but we'd look … normal. We'd been in the dark too long. Our physiology had adapted to those dank, damp dwellings. The others chased us away, called us monsters, and tried to end our lives. Of course we made the deal."

*Her stomach ached. Had the Skinwalker done this?*

"What does any of this have to do with me?"

"That spell birthed many things other than us and bound them tight by rules. Most of us can't walk in the day, and those able can't take exposure for extended periods of time. At least that used to be the case." He shook his head as he placed his hand on a flat panel. A green light scanned from the bottom to the top, and it opened. "Our minds are turning against us, crumbling under the weight of years at an alarming rate. The Weres no longer require the moon. They shift at will. Their whole hierarchy is turning upside down. The societies once ruled by the iron fists of alphas are engaged in a bloody civil war with an ex-council member who likes to make rogues." He waited for her to precede him through the door.

The images he depicted made up one giant ticking time-bomb that blotted out her impression of the building they were walking through.

"You are powerful enough to perform the spell again."

"Me? I've never done anything of that magnitude. Besides that, who has it? Because we don't. Are we even certain I'm the one?"

"It was predicted long ago by a very powerful Shaman. You are the firstborn from his line born in centuries who could do this. It will take more than power. The person needed to walk in the three worlds, not human or vampire, but a mixture of both with a bit of wolf. Your father has some Were in his lineage."

"So, a genetic anomaly. That's what all of this boils down to? I'm just the poor bastard who won the unlucky lottery." She gritted her teeth, careful not to push him too far. *We needed someone who could walk in both worlds. Not human, and not vampire.* It all lined up with what the SkinWalker showed her. Her stomach bubbled. *Will I turn evil like he did?* They crossed the stone floor room, and she caught glimpses of rows of wine racks filled with bottles.

"Please tell me that's fermented grapes."

"Partially." His face morphed and he rushed toward her.

She tossed her hands up. A powerful blast left her, throwing him across the room.

He chuckled. "Very good."

"What the hell was that?" she asked, high off adrenaline as she held her shield closely.

"The official start of training. If I gave you a warning, it wouldn't simulate real life."

She stared at his throat. "Vampires don't actually need to breathe, do they?"

"No. Why?"

*Because I think I might strangle you to death.*

"Morbid curiosity," she said dryly. She watched him warily, feeling like a customer in a haunted house waiting for the scare she knew could be around any corner.

"This isn't an estate. It's a castle." She took in the high stone walls, tapestries, and furniture she knew was older than her.

"Yes, I suppose this is not ordinary for you."

"And it is for you? How old are you?"

"Lesson number two. It's rude to ask a vampire his age." The cocky smirk made her huff as they continued through the castle.

*At least I'll be imprisoned in style and luxury.*

"Is this Hogwarts and today is my first day?" Keeta asked as they walked into the library.

"This is where we'll be when we aren't training," he replied, ignoring her tone.

"Why?"

"As you mentioned, we don't know what the actual spell was, or how to fix what's wrong. We've amassed everything we could on our history. Some were rumors and legends, but in each, we expected there to be a grain of truth."

She cast her gaze around the room. "And you expect me to sift through all of this?"

"I'll be assisting you. We're in this together." He walked over to the section they'd dedicated to their mission.

She laughed. "You expect me to start now?"

"I warned you in the plane we'd begin immediately."

"Listen, Robo Cop. I'm a human. I need food, and if you want me to function after everything that happened a hot shower, clean clothes, and coffee. You don't want to see me without coffee." She crossed her arms, and her magic crackled definitely around her. Her green eyes darkened.

He paused. "I've been in the company of my own kind a long time. Perhaps I've forgotten the way of things with your people."

"Uh, yeah. Your manners leave much to be desired."

"Careful witch," he growled, his eyes briefly flashing red.

"Or what? You need me."

"We can make this a miserable experience or a tolerable one," he said through gritted teeth.

"Do you mean I can bow down to you or retain some sense of who I was?" She tilted her head. "Because I choose me every time."

"I am trying to be nice to you."

"This is you *trying* to be nice? You must be a real piece of work then."

Her words hit their target. He was handling this all wrong. He paused, and put a chokehold on the beast inside, ready to respond to her challenge.

There was no time to persuade her to believe the truth. The only thing keeping her from jumping ship were the wards impeding her inability to access her powers. He had to change that, quickly. Back when he was alive, things were simple. He worked for the highest bidder, pledging loyalty to no one, and bedding wenches when the need arose. *That's why you landed in this position forever seeking penance.*

He never believed in the spiritual, had counted on going into the ground, and turning back to dust when he was killed. Thinking of the atrocities he'd committed, what he'd seen and done since that time, he snorted. Life was hell on Earth. *Talk about a kick to the bullocks.* Not a day went by that he didn't wonder about the fate of his soul.

By nature, he needed the life-giving substance from another to survive. Surely there could be no place in heaven for him. *Dante's Inferno* flickered in his mind.

*Blokes these days don't know how easy they have it.* The horrific words and pictures rattling around in his brain would scar them for life. The watered-down biblical teaching and right to choose still boggled his mind, and yet, they took it for granted. He often wondered what it'd be like to grow up in this time, free from all of the old teachings, expectations, and daily struggles to survive. *Now is not the time to get philosophical.* You can take the man out of the Renaissance— but you can't take the Renaissance out of the man.

"I am not used to dealing with humans in this capacity."

"Have you forgotten you used to be one?" She countered, narrowing her gaze. "Because that lame answer is not gaining any sympathy from me. You think this is difficult for you?" She grabbed the curly black locks that tumbled down her back and tugged. "I don't even recognize myself. I refuse to do anything else until I've had a moment to myself."

"Do you understand what's at stake?"

"I can't help anyone else if I'm drowning." The wards wavered under her burst of power. She frowned. "What is this?"

"Wards to keep you from overexerting yourself."

"How is this going to help me?"

He shrugged one shoulder casually, as if this were an everyday conversation. "They will lessen in time. It's a way to keep you from hurting yourself."

"And you, right? Don't leave that out."

Her arrogance angered him. "I am not so easily injured. You'd do well to remember that."

Balling his fists, he averted his gaze before the witch could see she got under his skin. "You want your time to collect yourself? Fine. Let me show you to your room." He spun around with the precision of a soldier and strode down the hall. The slap of her flat feet on the stone as she rushed to keep up with his pace made him smirk. He might have to play nice, but there was no need to placate her at every turn. He was a knight used to running things. He gave a command and expected it to be followed, not sassed and questioned. Her bravery could be seen as admirable if it didn't hinder his main objective.

"How am I supposed to remember my way back here? This place is like the Malfoy manor. I need a map or breadcrumbs."

"We share a bond. If I allow it, you have access to my memories."

"What kind of Sci-fi crap is this?" she asked. The panic in her voice was clear.

"You're a witch. Your will remains your own. I can't treat you like a puppet if that's what you're worried about. Think of the link as a bridge between us."

He touched her mental barrier and stopped. Respect meant asking. Pushing down his ire, he slowed his pace and looked down at her. "Allow me?"

"Okay." She twisted her fingers nervously.

Slipping through her barriers, he shared the castle layout.

"Oh." Her full red lips parted with a shaky sigh, and his mind wandered to places it shouldn't. Even swimming in his clothes, she was gorgeous with her coarse curls, bright green eyes, and a delicate heart-shaped face. A beautiful bronze maiden with curves he shouldn't notice and a warmth he hadn't experienced in a long time. People had a feel about them and he all but drowned in the bright light and heat she gave off.

Feeling like a voyeur, he cast his gaze downward and cleared his throat. "Better?"

"Yes. Thank you."

He nodded and continued to her room. Decorated in shades of pale green with a modernized bathroom en suite it was spacious and feminine … and close enough to his rooms to keep an eye on her, but far enough away to give her a semblance of privacy. Like a prickly cactus, if he held her too tightly, she bit back.

"You asked for time. I'll grant you that. We'll readjourn in the dining room in three hours. Tomorrow we'll begin training."

Her gaze bored into him, but he refused to meet her stare. She'd be no good to him closed off and cranky. They meshed like oil and water. He could do this to keep the peace.

Stopping in front of her quarters, he gave a slight bow. "You'll find everything you need inside."

She turned to speak, and he used his speed to escape her words, her scent, and her humanity. With every action, she showed him how far he'd drifted from being human. The ground brought back memories he'd stored in the back of his brain for a reason. He'd been a feral animal when Dregan first brought him here in a metal cage. Despite his best efforts, he fell down a rabbit hole and landed at the beginning of his rebirth.

Past

THE HOLY WATER LACED RUNGS burned his hands. He stumbled back from the bar, staring down at his blisters and burned skin.

"You will not act like as a savage here. Being turned on a battlefield with the stench of blood and death in the air would've driven any new fledgling into bloodlust. We won't hold that against you. However, if you can't get a hold of yourself, we will execute you. You understand what I am saying?"

Crewe snarled at the large, blond Viking with a long, wheat-colored braid and beard to match. Two braids stood out against his long beard. His brilliant blue gaze held a hint of battle lust he knew all too well as a mercenary knight. The authority sliced through the never-ending hunger.

"I'm hungry." His voice was garbled, guttural

"And you'll continue to be. There's nothing that completely slakes the thirst."

He clutched his stomach, rocking back and forth as the stabbing pains grew worse.

"You'll weather this, or go insane trying. There's nothing more anyone can do. It's up to you now whether you live or die. I saw you on the battlefield in action. Your reputation precedes you. You've the heart of a fighter. Use that to defeat the hunger." With that, they'd retreated, taking the light from the torches with him. The pain increased, and he curled into a ball. Moisture coated him. He touched his skin and came away with blood.

He could no longer sweat, yet he could do this? *What kind of fiend from hell have I become? Is this my punishment for all of the death I brought in wars waged?* His stomach clenched and he shook like a man with a fever. Rolling onto his stomach, he expelled a red river. The metallic scent enraged him. He lapped at the puddle only to oust it again. Disgusted, he pushed himself away from the area and crawled toward the other side of the cage. Convulsing, he watched the ghosts of his enemy fill the space, sneering down as he relived the killing blows he'd dealt. Shame kicked in as his life played in front of him. He spent a lifetime chasing coin and never helped anyone for no gain. He lent his lances to any cause that gained him profit. It was a soulless existence. Perhaps this was his punishment.

Time blurred. A brilliant light drew his attention to the opposite side of his stone prison. The light sped closer, pausing just outside of the cage. He squinted, and the light dimmed, revealing a woman. White wings stretched out behind her. Sleek, black hair tumbled to her waist. She carried a large broadsword and wore a shiny metal helmet.

"You were chosen for greater things, young warrior. Agree to fulfill a mission, and I will take away your pain."

"Anything," he croaked.

"Now is not the time. You will know when." She knelt beside his cage and touched him with icy hands that soothed his broken mind as he eased into a blissful unawareness.

## Present

For centuries he'd believed the woman to be a hallucination. Now he wasn't sure. Was this what he'd agreed to? Time wasn't on their side, and she made no attempt to hide her dislike for him, nor he for her. They didn't have time for this pettiness. He could feel the urgency pressing in on him. Things wouldn't remain stable for much longer. Returning to the dungeon, he stood in the spot where he woke a new person, with a new purpose. Dregan taught him everything he knew. Raised him like a father would a son and gave him a reason to live—keeping the law and maintaining the secrecy that kept them all safe.

He couldn't fail him, or his people. This was his chance to right the wrongs he'd done in his lifetime. Then maybe he could die in peace. He'd seen too much death and experienced the passing of time far beyond his years. He went from horses to airplanes, and candlelight to electricity, and watched everyone he knew die along with their seed until he could no longer stand to watch over his own bloodline. There was nothing so bad as truly knowing you didn't belong. Languages, mannerisms, and society at large were vastly changed, and he was tired of fighting. This was his swan song.

# Chapter Four

KEETA

SHE KNEW THIS CAVE. A chill settled over her skin and she rubbed her arms as she spun in a circle, taking in the rough walls lit by the flickering flames of the fire. *Why am I back here?* A lonely howl rended the air. Spinning around, she saw the large, gray wolf slink inside of the mouth of the cave. Tense, she waited. The wolf turned into the Native American Skin Walker with a gray pelt draped over his shoulders. Today he wore only a loincloth and moccasins. His skin glistened with sweat, and his dark hair was pulled back in a single braid.

"Why am I here?" she asked, softly.

"To see. The Nations must come together."

"The Native American Tribes?"

"No. The wolf, the vampire, and the witches." He stepped closer, and she took a step back. He had an oily, dark aura. As if the things he'd dabbled in lingered.

"Here you are not in control." He grabbed her wrist. "You will see and then you'll understand." Gripping her chin, he forced her mouth open, then opened his mouth. She struggled against his iron grasp. Red smoke rolled from between his lips and into hers. The taste of ashes, wood, and blood flooded her mouth. She gagged as she swallowed the mixture down and he released her. The room spun. She swayed on her feet. Sweat beaded on her brow, and her stomach turned.

"Sit down. The vision will come to you soon." Her knees weakened, and she landed heavily on her butt on the ground. He began to chant, throwing sage leaves on the fire as he poured water onto heated stones, causing steam. The smoke filled her lungs, stung her eyes, and made her sluggish. The background fell away, and she landed headlong into a vision.

She stood in the background, a shadow no one else noticed in the clearing. The people shed their crude clothing. Doeskin breeches and dresses with fringe. Once nude, their bodies began to contort. She cried out as bones cracked, and backs bent at unnatural angles. Their faces elongated as they grew muzzles. Hair sprouted out of pores and their forms twisted and changed. A large wolf threw back its head and released a howl. The others joined. *The alpha.* His eyes were a deep amber. He stood proudly as the others rested on their belly, always keeping their heads lower than him as they peered up at him with respect and adulation.

He lifted his muzzle in the air. His black nose twitched from left to right, and he released a low growl that made her want to pee her pants. The wolf's hackles rose, and his people flanked him, ready for his command. She took a step back in response to his aggression. A familiar gray wolf padded into the wooded area. *No.* The white wolf stood his ground; ears back, body tense. The gray wolf sprang forward. The white wolf batted him away with a powerful paw.

The gray wolf recovered quickly, nipping at the white wolf's flank. They tumbled onto the ground, biting and tussling as each attempted to assert dominance. They moved to their hind legs, exchanging blows as they struck at each other's throats. Blood coated the white wolf's pelt. She couldn't tell whom it belonged to. A whimper rung out in the clearing. The gray wolf had latched onto the white wolf's throat. He shook him back and forth like a rag doll. Crimson spread along his fur. The dying wolf was tossed to the ground, and the gray wolf stalked to him. Burying his muzzle into the white wolf's chest, he dug through the flesh and devoured his heart. The darkened muzzle was washed red in the moonlight.

"Oh, God." She covered her mouth with her hand.

The pack lowered their bodies in submission, and the gray wolf's eyes glinted a sickly yellow. The howl he unleashed sounded more like a roar that disturbed the forest and made the ground quake beneath them. The unearthly sound sent the creatures in the surrounding area running, and put an ache in her gut.

Nature itself protested the imbalance. Clouds blotted out the full moon. A crack of thunder proceeded lighting that downed a tree nearby. The wind howled, shaking the branches, stirring up leaves, and making the wolves antsy. The sky broke, and hail beat down, sending the wolves running off in search of shelter from the baseball-sized hail. She locked eyes with the gray wolf, and for a moment their minds merged. She gagged on the metallic taste of blood and the lust for power. She woke choking on the memory of the blood coating her mouth.

Throwing the covers off her bed, she breathed heavily. The hunger for flesh lingered. Disgusted mentally, but unable to retain control of her body, she sniffed. A delectable scent filled her nostrils. Her stomach growled. She rose from the bed, tracking the aroma. Moving out of her room and down the hall, she made her way into the opposite wing. Breathing heavily, she leaned toward the wooden door that barred her from the prize. The door swung, and she stepped inside, walking past Crewe to reach the source. A glass of burgundy liquid rested on the table in front of the window. She paused, running her finger around the rim. The high-pitched tone soothed her.

"Nakeeta?"

She glanced at the shirtless vampire, licking her lips as she admired the sculpted masterpiece molted with scars.

"What are you doing?"

She returned her attention to the glass. "What is this? It smells delicious." Grasping the stem, she lifted it to the moonlight, swirling it to release the aroma. Unable to resist, she brought the glass to her lips. The thick, cool substance coated her mouth and slid down her throat. Licking the stray drops from her lips, she froze. "Oh my God. What did I just do?" Dropping the empty glass, she trembled as her body grew hot. Her body lifted from the ground and jerked. She gave under the weight of the pressure building.

She woke among shards of glass on the ground. Slivers of glass bit into her skin. Crewe knelt in a defensive position. Distended fangs hung past his lips and dripped blood. Her throat stung. She brought her palm up, shocked when she felt a wet, warm substance. Pulling it away, she spotted blood.

"What happened?"

"You were in a trance. I wasn't sure what would happen if I didn't snap you out of it," he growled.

"So, you bite me?"

"Be happy I didn't break your neck. You flung me across the room with no warning. What triggered that?"

"A dream. No ... a vision."

"About?"

"How the spell was weakened." She launched into the dream, and he listened intently.

"So the Skinwalker wanted more power, and he garnered it by any means necessary."

"Greed is always the downfall of those who seek power." *This is where my own weakness comes from. It's in my blood.* She'd ingested blood, a life-giving substance taken from who knew where. What did it mean for her magic, or hell her soul? The glass rattled against the stone floor.

"Calm down."

"I'm trying."

"Try harder."

Furious, she directed her anger toward the stoic vampire who'd risen to his feet. He flew against the wall, landing with a sickening crack. Eyes red, he charged a blur at the top speed. She blinked and found herself beside the exit.

"The witch has new tricks. Let's see how long you can keep it up." Her heart pounded in her chest as she gave chase. She sensed him behind her, a silent predator stalking as it waited for the right moment to strike. He rushed past her. *Too close for comfort.* She froze him in place. His animalistic snarl pierced her to the core. Eyes scarlet, and features twisted into something otherworldly, this was the hunger controlling the man.

"Run." Distorted, his voice acted like the bullet from a starting gun at the beginning of a race. She fled out of the hallway to the maze outside. The damp night air did nothing to calm her, and she hardly felt the cool ground on her skin and bare feet. Disappearing into the high, green walls of shrubbery, she dove through hedges and doubled back to dead ends, spreading her scent to throw him off her trail. Despite the darkness, she saw clearly. *Add better vision to the list of freakish changes.* Every day she moved further away from what and who she once was.

A low, evil laugh filled the maze. "Do you think you can escape me?" The amusement in his voice terrified her. Suddenly, she missed the tight-laced prick persona.

The top of the hedge in front of her exploded as he leapt over the wall. The ground shook with his impact. He knelt in front of her. His head snapped back.

"I will always find you. My blood flows in your veins." She blinked, and he moved in front of her. His minty breath caressed her face, stirring the tendrils sticking to her forehead. Tunnel vision took over as she met his crazed stare. A link opened between them, and she experienced his tentative hold on sanity. Wincing, she pressed her hands against her ears as the weight of memories gathered over time, and the insatiable lust for blood drove her to her knees.

Piles of bodies rested in a pool of blood. Their throats were viciously torn, and their faces were twisted in an odd combination of pain and ecstasy.

Stumbling over a severed head, she moved through the hellish landscape of what once was a quaint village. The walls of the stone structures were splattered with blood. A smear from a bloody hand chilled her to the bone. *What happened here?* A shape moved in from the darkness. Nude, he was covered in blood. His scarlet eyes stood out in the night. Crazed he rummaged through the piles of bodies, sniffing each before he discarded the carcass carelessly. A moan came from the bottom of the pile near her. He sped toward the sound.

"No." She wielded her power like a knife, severing their connection.

Crewe stumbled back. "What did you do, witch?"

"I-I don't know." She shook her head.

"Stay out of my head."

"Believe me I'd like to!"

"You think you can control me with your pitiful attempt at mind control."

"Do you think I wanted to see you gorge yourself on humans?" she cried.

He stiffened. "What did you say?"

"I saw what you did to that village. Jesus. You're an animal, aren't you? Is that why they sent me with you? Because you'll do whatever it takes to keep me in line?"

She met his blown-out pupils, and she stopped mid-sentence. His chest moved up and down rapidly, and he balled his fists. Tilting his head back he roared. Fear blossomed in her chest like a night flower opening its petals. Veins popped up in his neck and he locked his vision on her. His nostrils flared. He took a menacing step toward her.

"Stop." She placed her hands on his chest, and the world shattered.

## CREWE

HE SPUN IN A CIRCLE, panicking as the bright rays of the sun blinded his sensitive eyes and warmed his skin. His jaw dropped as he swept his gaze over the area, seeking shelter. Soon his skin would blister and burn. Palm trees filled the area behind him. He darted for the shade the large, green leaves provided. The scent of salty sea air filled his nostrils. *Did she teleport us?*

"Witch," he bellowed, "what have you done?"

"I don't know." Turning, he found her a few yards away. Brow furrowed she reached out to touch the rough bark of a tree.

"You'd better figure it out soon, or you'll learn firsthand what the sun can do to a vampire."

"I thought the spell was lessening."

He rushed forward, slamming her body back against the tree. Placing his hand beside her head, he leaned down. His hand itched to wrap around her throat. "You have a smart mouth. Careful it doesn't bite off more than you can chew."

"And yet you don't come out of our encounters unscathed, do you?" she asked breathily.

Her lush curves pressed into him, and her sultry scent assaulted his nose. *Brave little thing.* "Fix it, witch."

"How can I think with you literally breathing down my neck?"

"You're lucky I'm not ripping it out."

"Then you'd never get out of here."

He pushed away from her and growled. Sniffing the air, he wrinkled his nose, and he shook his head. "This place is wrong."

"Why?"

"It smells wrong, artificial."

"I don't think we're really here." She closed her eyes and stilled.

Entranced, he watched her search her surroundings. Her power reached out, brushing up against him as it left her going out to do her bidding. Dark curls blew away from her face. Her full, red lips parted as she inhaled. He licked his lips. *Tasty morsel.*

Her eyes popped open. "This is a dream state. Similar to what one will experience in a vision."

"You brought us into your mind?"

"I brought us somewhere."

"Speak plainly fast, witch."

"I think we're on an astral plane. It's why the sun isn't affecting you."

"Why would you bring us here?"

"I …" She shook her head. "I don't know."

He grunted. "How do we go back?"

He couldn't tear his gaze from the sun. It'd been so long since he saw the golden ball and felt it's soothing rays on his flesh. "I've never done anything like this before."

"You tend to say that a lot around me."

"What can I say? You bring out the best in me." She shrugged and wiggled her toes, drawing his attention to the fact that she was barefoot.

He sneered. "Since this mess is yours to clean up, what do you suggest we do?"

"Explore and see if we can find a clue to why we're here or how to get back."

He gritted his teeth. "Walk."

"Older men usually have better manners," she muttered.

Exposed, angered, and out of his element, he longed to silence her with his hands. With the transition came a distance from control and humanity. The years chipped away at the sanctity of life, until it was nothing to snuff out the flickering candle that glowed inside every creature. The irreparable damage that came with watching everything you knew and loved fall away and die calloused the soul. It made rough places from those meant to be smooth and tender. He'd stopped thinking of himself as a member of the human race long ago, but the feel of the sun on his face shook something loose inside of him.

*It's not real.* He chanted the words in his head as he scanned the area for signs of a threat. The powdery white sand, soothing sounds of the ocean to the left, and tropical palm trees with coconuts were a mirage. There was no going back to what he'd once been. It'd be foolishness to hope otherwise.

"Why the beach?" He frowned at the hot sun. A native of England, he'd never been one for tropical weather. Give him an overcast sky, brisk chill, and rain.

"I'm not sure. I haven't been to a beach in ages."

He froze. "If you're not controlling this, who is?"

Her lower lip trembled, and she shook her head.

The rumble of thunder sounded in the distance. He turned to face the horizon and saw a group of gray clouds quickly approaching. Lightning flashed, too close for comfort.

"Move faster," he snapped, returning his gaze to her.

"To where?"

"Someplace farther from the water. I'm not willing to test the theory on what happens if we're gravely injured here."

A streak of bright light spiderwebbed close to the shore. Placing a hand on the small of her back, he guided her deeper into the lush jungle. A prickling sensation traveled down his spine. He scanned the area once more. They were being hunted.

"What's wrong?" she whispered.

"Nothing."

"I can feel how concerned you are."

"I'm not certain. A feeling of foreboding is urging me to—"

The sand beside them exploded. He snatched her up and dodged to the left. White hot heat morphed sand into a quartz sculpture that stuck out of the ground. He glanced at the woman in his arms.

Letting instinct take over he continued to speed his way in a zig-zag pattern, staying ahead of the strikes as they moved to the heart of the landscape. In the distance, three waterfalls tumbled down a cliff that led to a flowing source of water. Dense forestry pressed in on either side, creating the perfect cover for a would-be attacker. Senses on alert, he focused.

"Oh my god. Crewe." Her voice shook. "Look at the water."

He turned to see the white spray had turned obsidian.

"She's coming."

"Who?"

"The Priestess. No matter what I do, I can't escape her. She's tainted my soul, and I'll never get clean." Her voice cracked, and a sob broke through.

A figure, darker than the black surface, began to emerge from the choppy waters. Rooted to the spot, he found himself unable to move. Straining to break the hold he growled low in his throat as the feminine form continued to rise. Dark tar-like substance dripped off the shapeless face.

"Fight her, witch," he snapped.

Black smoke snaked from the creature along the ground, covering it like a dense fog. His chest tightened, and he felt the press of power as the fog engulfed them. The fog swirled around him, forming an impenetrable tornado. He choked on the scent of decay, gripping Keeta as tight against his chest as he could manage. A sense of weightlessness settled over him. He knew no more.

❈ ❈

HE OPENED HIS EYES AND groaned as he moved away from the hard, cold slab he lay across. Sitting up, he jerked back, stunned. He'd been resting on a stone slab in front of a weathered off-white mausoleum. Stone angels with praying hands and cherub faces mocked him from either side. Rising, he took in the neat row of tombs and mausoleums. *Why am I in a cemetery? Where's Keeta?* The scent of magic perfumed the air.

He could sense her through the bond close by and terrified. Following her signature, he sped through the rows of above ground graves. He stopped short of a mass of people clad in black around a crude altar. Markings etched in white chalk were the center of the group of woman and men. A tall woman swallowed down alcohol from a bottle and spit it onto the ground as the others changed. Their bodies began to move to the rhythm they kept. The dance started slowly and picked up along with the tempo. She jerked like a marionette controlled by a puppet master as she called out in Creole.

He spotted Keeta on the other side of the circle watching as another version of herself approached the woman with a chicken. Black blood magic, the kind that gave power at a cost most weren't willing to pay. Her eyes were alight with joy, and her full lips were painted black and curved into a wicked grin.

"I didn't understand what it truly meant," she whispered too low for anyone other than a vampire to hear. "I was young and arrogant. I thought I could control it. The thing is you don't control black magic. It controls you. It's like an addiction. Yes. It makes you more powerful, but like any substance, you have to do more and more to get the same high."

The former Keeta held up the chicken, and the woman ran her sharp blade over its throat. The blood dripped onto the etchings. The wind picked up in the cemetery. The white chalk glowed red with power.

The Priestess sprinkled more libations on the ground and lit a thick cigar. She blew smoke on the offering pile and added coins. As the chanting continued, an aura of power rose.

"We called him, Papa Leba, and he answered."

Crewe watched transfixed as a cloud crept over the moon. The candles flickered out. The wicks relit, burning black, and a shadowy figure stood in the center. Broad shoulders, a wide-brimmed hat, and golden eyes were the only impression he could take as the being swept through the crowd touching each of them. One by one their heads fell back and they swayed slightly back and forth in a trance. Each lifted from the ground. An electric green haze surrounded them like a cocoon. They slowly spun in a circle faster and faster until they were a blur.

The ground shook, and a plant holder exploded behind them. All at once they fell to the ground in a heap.

The Priestess was the first to stir. A husky laugh spilled from her thin lips. Despite the bell-like quality, he felt like he'd stepped on a pile of slithering snakes. She stood and sauntered over to the blood in the circle. Sweeping her finger through the blood, she moved to Keeta and painted her lips.

"You are bound to me now, servant." Repeating the process, she sank her magical hooks into the other nine people.

"That was the start of hell on Earth."

"What did she do to you?"

"Infected us like a drug dealer giving the first taste. It took me nearly a year to break free. I lost everything, and I had to start over from scratch. Even worse, I had an inclination for the darkness. They saw me when they once wouldn't have. Once you look into the darkness, the darkness looks back."

"You liked it."

"Worse. I loved it. I had to walk away and never look back, and even then … I have weak moments. Living uninhibited by rules or a moral compass was intoxicating. The power I attained—" She licked her lips.

He felt a stirring he ignored. Her nostrils flared, and the scent of desire teased his nose.

"Why are we here at this moment?"

She shook her head and lowered her gaze. "It's my greatest shame."

"We've all done things we aren't proud of."

"I didn't say that."

He scowled. "I heard you clearly."

"I didn't say it out loud. I thought it."

He blinked. "Because we haven't had enough surprises."

Her peal of hysteric laughter tugged at his protective instincts. He flinched. It was wrong seeing the Spitfire like this. Their bond bid him fix her.

"We're okay."

"Okay? We don't even know where we are or why. I'm reliving the worst period of my life, and it's not even done yet. God." She shuddered and gestured wildly toward the scene playing itself out like a horror movie. It chilled him to see her stand, eyes dull and vacant as she watched the Priestess like a zombie awaiting command. His hackles rose. Keeta didn't belong to this magic wielding maniac. Her place was at his side. The bond flared. He wrapped an arm around her and drew her to him.

"This is your past. It's a part of who you are, but it's not everything. If I've learned anything, it's this. What we did is not the sum of who we are. The good, bad, and in between meld together to create our present being. You can't crucify yourself over one mistake—"

"It was a big one," she stated, interrupting him.

"I assure you whatever wrongs you perceive mine are worse." Words left his lips before he could silence them. "The term freelance came from people like me. Hired knights who fought for any cause that paid coin. I lead the life of a soulless bastard, with no fealty. Now, I'll pay for it for eternity."

She peered up at him wide-eyed. "You can't believe that."

"I know that." Pity came through the link, burning him like acid. He batted away the emotion, slamming the link between them down. "Save your pity for someone who needs it."

"You don't get to tell me how to feel."

*That's the fire I want to see.* He'd take the irritation over her bought of self-loathing and weakness. He needed her strong, and alert.

"Do you feel that?" she whispered.

"Feel what?"

She shivered. "The cold." A lone snowflake drifted down from the sky. The cemetery melted away like crayon on a hot summer day. The imagery streaked, smeared, and swirled together. He blinked, swaying drunkenly as his senses were overwhelmed.

# Chapter Five

### Keeta

Teeth chattering, she rubbed her arms as she wiggled her toes. Ankle deep in the frozen white precipitation, she was out of her element. A tree provided partial shelter in the forest above a crude tent erected a few feet away from a circle of stones that housed a fire in the middle. Sensing Crewe's approach, she turned. "What is this place?"

"The worst winters of my life."

"Why are you squatting?" She frowned. *Shouldn't he be in a castle with a room and servant wenches falling all over him?* "I thought you were a knight?"

"I was. We were required to provide for ourselves during our travel." Her eyes widened. Food was not plentiful, or easily accessible in this time. This put a whole new view on knighthood. "I was on my way to the nearest town to seek out work when winter hit early, so I found shelter. The tree provided me with some shelter from the elements, and there's hunting here."

"Hunting?" Images of the beginning of Bambi ran through her head.

"Yes. Unless you live in a castle, where it's done for the entire building, it's the way of things. Food spoils easily. Crops aren't genetically altered and guaranteed to yield produce, so you eat what you can when you can get it. Being picky wasn't a luxury we possessed." He moved to the tent, lifted the flap, and glanced inside. "My older self isn't here yet, so he's probably out hunting," he said more to himself than her. Removed and stoic, he was near impossible to read. The bond helped, but he was fast growing accustomed and blocking her as much as he could.

Apprehension slipped through to her.

"What's wrong?"

"We can feel in this place." He spoke quietly.

"And?" She shook her head, lost.

"It's not a time I wish to relive or have you experience with me."

"Crewe. What aren't you telling me?"

"I nearly froze to death and starved out here."

"How long do we have?"

"I don't know what stage we're at," he said softly. "Get inside. You're cold. It's easier to keep warm when there are two people." Frightened, she proceeded him into the small tent.

"This is in our head, though, right? We can't really be hurt here …"

"You know as well as I do, the mind is a powerful thing."

She swallowed and huddled near the small fire in the center of the tent.

"Come here." Crewe knelt down, pulled back a thick pelt, and climbed into the mound of bedding he had. "Take your gown off—"

"What?" she squawked.

"Body heat." He stared her down, and she shook her head. "I can't generate my own heat, but I can regulate with yours. We need to dry your feet and get you under the pelts and warm."

"No." She shivered.

"I'm trying to save your bloody life, not sneak a peek."

She cringed at the ire in his voice. Her hands shook as she tried to grab the hem of her dress. Clumsy fingers refused to cooperate. Gently, he pushed her hands aside.

"Raise your arms." He peeled the nightgown off with clinical precision. Keeping his eyes averted, he knelt, drying off her feet. He laid the gown out to dry by the fire while she slipped into the soft pile he'd turned down for her. She tucked the top layer under her arms.

"Let me see your feet." She'd never experienced temperatures like this. It was more than being in the dead of winter with improper clothing. Her bones ached, and her fingers and toes tingled. Stiff, she complied with his command without protest.

He took her feet in his hands and began a massage. She moaned as feeling began to return to the numb blocks of ice. His thumbs moved over the balls of her feet, hitting pressure points she hadn't realized she possessed as he worked his way down.

"Can you still feel them?"

"Yes, they're tingling."

"Good. It means you still have circulation. Move over."

She lifted the fur, and he slipped in beside her. His sandalwood scent surrounded her. Her teeth chattered.

"Come here." He pulled her to lay on his chest and rubbed her back vigorously. Burying her nose in his neck, she focused on the rise and fall of his chest. He didn't need to breathe, but the human habit seemed to be one they all kept. In a strange, unpredictable place, he was her constant. Bit by bit the cold receded, and her lids grew heavy.

"Rest for now. Soon, I'll leave to find us food."

Exhausted from the emotional and physical roller coaster, she allowed her guard to lower enough to escape into sleep where her stomach wasn't eating itself, and she wasn't in danger of freezing to death.

"Nakeeta." A warm hand rubbed her back, and she snuggled closer to the well-built chest holding up her head. Nuzzling her nose into the smooth expanse of skin covered in fine hairs, she inhaled. He smelled like sandalwood but underneath the skin, flowing through his veins, she caught a top note of strawberries.

"You smell like strawberries," she mumbled.

"Well, that's a first. You have to get up love. I need to hunt."

The accent hit her like cold water. She sat up, untangling her limbs from his. Her face heated. She'd lowered her guard and gotten too comfortable.

"What's a little skin on skin contact between bonded?" He arched a thick blond brow, and she shook her head and balled her hands into fists. Her life was no longer her own. She needed to maintain control over everything she could.

"You are not my prisoner, but we are in this together, and it is my duty to care for you."

"So you say."

"So Dregan says."

Her heart dropped at the mention of his boss. This was a business transaction. She'd forgotten that.

He tucked her chin with his forefinger, forcing her to meet his gaze. "Don't put words in my mouth. We're complicated."

"Don't be nice now that you feel sorry for me." She sniffed and turned her head away. "Go. I'll be fine."

"If the other me comes back, I don't believe he'll see you. Just like in your memories."

She gave a curt nod.

He sighed and shook his head before digging to find clothing stored away in a soft saddle bag. His back muscles rippled as he pulled on layers of crudely made homespun clothing. There was no harm admitting he was a good-looking man with a nice body. She wasn't blind. Shifting in her pallet, she felt apprehension at being separated.

"Don't worry. I'll be swift."

*What if he doesn't come back? What if we're trapped here in an endless loop of suffering?* Her thoughts ran from the mundane to the fantastical. She knew witches could be powerful, but the things she'd been able to do recently blew her mind. Most never reached this level of capabilities, for a good reason. The universe kept a balance. Not everyone was meant to wield this. Hell, she was only chosen because of a genetic lottery.

Crewe crouched down in front of her and took her hands in his. "I will return for you always. The bond joins us. I am not your sire. But I do feel responsible for you. You are the closest I've ever come or will come to procreating."

"What does that mean for a vampire?"

"That you are unique to me." He squeezed her hand. She sensed a deeper truth through their bond but refrained from digging. Now was not the time.

"I'll try to figure out a way to get us home while you're away." Later she'd ask. Right now, they had to get the hell out of here. Worst case scenario, they'd end up lost here while their bodies atrophied back home. *Can a vampire even do that?* Clearing her mind, she inhaled, letting the sandalwood and strawberries scent of Crewe mingle with her own to become a new normal. She'd been a woman divided ever since she woke in the hospital. It was always the kiss of death for magic.

"Thou wast sent here for a reason."

Keeta's eyes popped open, and she found a fair-skinned woman with pitch black hair that stopped at her ankles in two braids and honey-colored eyes that glowed with power. Her red dress with gold trim and peasant sleeves matched the Old English she spoke. This was no ordinary witch.

"Who are you?" she whispered, afraid of the answer.

"A distant ancestor sister. Blessed be, sister. I am known as Morgan to some."

Her eyes widened. *Le Fay?* "Blessed be, crone." She bent, giving a bow.

"You are meant to learn."

"Learn what?" she asked, flabbergasted.

"Thou must figure that out for thy self. You are the key. We are here to help guide you, but we will not take away your free will or the natural order of things. No one should have that kind of power. You will be the deciding factor for this generation. Choose wisely."

"B-but I don't know what I'm d-doing?" she stuttered, shaking her head, her brows pinched in confusion.

"Neither did we." She winked and disappeared as seamlessly as she'd arrived.

"Suddenly I feel like I'm trapped inside an episode of *Lost*," she whispered. Rubbing her chilled arms, she tried to remember exactly what they were doing before they were transported. Arguing was their default mode. If they were stranded here for that, they'd never leave. Massaging her throbbing temples, she returned to square one. She tried to focus, but was distracted by her rumbling belly. Hunger pains made her grunt. Clutching her belly, she glanced at the tent flap anxiously.

*How long has he been gone?* She shifted in her nest. A few hours ago, all she wanted to do was escape him. Now she couldn't help but reach out to touch him through their connection. He as hungry, frustrated, and tired. Her shoulders slumped dejectedly. Slipping into his mind she saw through his eyes. Icicles hung off the low hanging branches weighed down by the snow. The snow was bare of tracks, and the forest was unusually silent.

Nothing stirred. The scents were all old, and any edible things were long dead. He pressed on, moving farther away. She could feel the red rage creeping up on him. The hunger would soon demand to be sated. If he didn't feed, it would force his hand. As he continued to search, his hold on control slipped.

"Stop. Come back." If they had to do this, it would be on her terms.

"I haven't found anything yet."

"And you won't if you keep ignoring what you need."

"I won't feed on you."

"What exactly do you plan on living off then? At least one of us has a viable food source." She tensed. The thought of being drank from wasn't sexy. It reminded her of parasites.

"I can feel how uncomfortable you are about this."

"This is a necessity. You are the stronger, more capable of us. We need you well."

"We'll talk when I return."

Her stomach tightened with nervousness and excitement. She sat on the back of her heels and held the furs to her. Butterflies danced in her stomach as she sensed his nearness. The flap opened, and his scarlet gaze met hers.

"I can't hold off much longer.

"Don't."

"It'll hurt if I don't do it right." His voice was distorted, but she felt no fear. A deep desire to care for him sent waves of calm coursing through her. He held himself away from her, shrinking against the flap.

"You took care of me earlier. Now let me take care of you."

"I don't think you understand what you're offering."

"Yes, I do. The bond works both ways." She tilted her head to the side.

His nostrils flared, and his fangs distended. He shuffled toward her in a trance-like state. Kneeling beside her, he ran his nose over her pulse point.

"You smell like freshly squeezed grapefruit. Mouthwatering, light, and refreshing." He trailed his tongue down her neck. She moaned, stunned by his action. "Let me make this feel good for you."

Her mouth went dry. Her stomach clenched. She was playing with fire. He nipped at her flesh, and she let her head fall back. "That's it. Relax." His tongue swiped across her artery. "I just want a little sip." He peppered kisses, nipping, sucking. She breathed shakily and gripped his shirt. His sharp fangs brushed her skin, once, twice, and he sank in. Her back arched. Pleasure flooded her body. She sank into the bond that exploded with color and emotions. For a brief moment, she connected with the man beneath the vampirism. Going back wouldn't be an option.

## CREWE

HE PULLED BACK WITH A mouthful of her sweet blood. Ingesting the warm substance, he licked his lips. Biting his own wrist, he held it up to her lips.

"Drink." She shook her head. Ignoring her weak protest, he placed his wrist to her lips. "It will tide you over." Her full lips parted, and he groaned as she sucked on the wound, taking him into her. Unable to keep his hands to himself, he stroked her hair, weaving his fingers into her curls.

This was the closest he'd allowed himself to be to another person since he turned. The desire to be held and accepted slammed into him like a lance. Shaken, he pulled back. A chink in the armor could be his downfall. *But what a way to go.* Death was an event he stopped fearing long ago. At this point, it'd be a relief.

*What happens if you've found a new reason to live?* The small voice echoed in the empty chamber that once housed his heart and compassion. Thrown off his game, he studied her. Her skin glowed, and her eyes were a bright violet. Parted red lips tempted him to think like a man.

"Are you okay?" The air around them grew electric. He held her closer. Sparks explode around them like golden fireworks. He sheltered her body, holding her tight as the bottom dropped out of his stomach, and the tent blurred. His stomach turned, and he found himself back in his body in the castle. Their bodies were in the exact same place as they had been.

"We're back." It felt like a lifetime had passed. Warily, he took a step back. The bond between them pulsed with life and use.

"You feel different."

"We exchanged blood. It strengthened the bond."

"It was in our head," she said softly.

He licked his lips and tasted her lingering flavor. "I'm not so sure."

Placing a hand on her neck, she brushed her fingers over the fading red marks. She ran her tongue over her teeth. "I can still taste you."

He stifled the moan that wanted to escape. "And I you."

"She said we were sent there for a reason."

"Who said?"

"The witch who appeared to me while you were gone. She said we'd been sent there to learn a lesson."

"So, you didn't send us there?" He bit the inside of his cheek, keeping his temper in check. She shut down when she felt threatened.

"I don't think so. There are powerful forces at work. They want to see us succeed, but they refuse to take away our free will."

"Who is this witch who can manipulate time and space?"

"Morgan Le Fey."

"She was a fictional character."

"You and I know more than most that there's a grain of truth in every legend. We're fighting for balance. I know we've spoken about it, but ..." She trailed off, shaking her head. "I'm ready to begin training now."

"After you've eaten."

She arched a brow. The shock that spread through their bond agitated him. "I've fed from you. I need to make sure you're properly taken care of."

"Right. We wouldn't want to hurt the mission."

Her words made him frown.

"I'll change and meet you in the dining room." She turned, and he felt chilled.

*What just happened?* He reached out and grabbed her. "Wait." Her back stiffened. "What are you doing?"

"Playing my part. It's what you wanted, right?"

"I thought we'd reached an understanding," he said, genuinely confused about her hot and cold behavior.

"Did we?"

"Nakeeta. I don't wish to be at odds with you."

"I don't know which is the real you," she blurted.

"I don't understand what you mean."

"Are you the uptight general with the stick up his ass, or the kind man who helped me survive a frigid winter? I don't like not knowing where I stand. I made that mistake once. It almost proved to be a grave error."

"You would compare me to that witch?"

"No." She winced, and he felt her regret. "I'm calling you an unknown factor."

"What would you have me do? Pledge my fealty to you and our cause? Come?" He tugged her gently and started toward the house.

"Where are we going?"

"To the chapel to perform the ceremony."

"You don't have to do that."

"And yet if I don't you will not be put at ease. I understand what it means to promise your loyalty to one person. I did not do this in life, so I shall do it in this undead existence, and then I will no longer entertain any of your doubt."

Her heartbeat kicked up a notch, but she stopped protesting.

They walked inside the chapel, and he glanced up at the intricate archways. Respect and awe-filled him as they walked between the seated area where the Royals would've sat during services. He'd had a long enough time to ponder the idea of religion. He couldn't say he bought into the concept of a Caucasian being floating on the cloud judging every moment, but there was a greater power. A force that tried to keep the balance and punished the wrong. He could buy into that. Reading the bible, he prayed that the forgiveness would be offered when he closed his eyes for the final time.

"This is the chapel where the royal family would attend church on Sundays. The priest would come to them."

"Its such a foreign concept for us Americans. Royalty, servants, and hierarchy."

"There's much more freedom now, but there's also chaos that comes along with not enough structure."

"Which do you think is better?" she asked in a hushed tone as they approached the stone altar.

"I don't think there's a right answer." He took her hands in both of his. "Fealty is a promise of service to the powers that be. It was believed that man called down punishment from the Lord himself if he spoke falsely. I'm not sure that I buy into the traditional concept of God, but I do believe in a higher power. So, we will swear to that."

"O-okay." Her voice warbled.

"Let's kneel." They sank to their knees in front of each other. "This will be our oath to one another."

"You know an oath with a witch is no small thing, right? It's another form of binding."

"I find I don't mind getting in deeper with you, Keeta." His words shocked them both; he could feel her surprise through the bond. Things were changing between them.

"I promise on my faith that I will in the future be faithful to Nakeeta Alves, never cause her harm nor practice deceit against her." He could feel the strands of magic weaving around them, binding them closer. He grimaced as she slipped through the cracks and spaces he'd sealed off from everyone else. The feel of human emotions overwhelmed him.

"Y-your turn."

"I don't know your last name," she said with a shaky laugh.

"Gresham."

"I promise on my faith that I will in the future be faithful to Crewe Gresham, never cause him harm nor practice deceit against him."

Her words wrapped around his heart and tightened. A jolt of electricity swept through him. Silvery white ropes of magic wound around them. His skin tingled. Her heart synched with his, and they breathed as one. Resting his forehead against hers, he allowed peace that long eluded him to enter his soul. This slip of a girl with a wicked tongue was altering him from the inside out as surely as his blood was doing to her.

BEING INSIDE OF HER BRAIN allowed him to train her more effectively.

"We're going to try something different today. The best training is tailored to the person. So we're going to play a game."

"A game?" She looked at him skeptically.

"Yes, capture the flag."

She glanced around. "With what teams?"

"Just us. You get the flag from me, and we'll call it a day."

"What's the catch?"

"No catch. Use everything you can to get the flag from me and take it to the center of the maze." He took the white flag from his pocket and waved it. She shot forward, and he spun, sending her stumbling toward the maze.

"You didn't think it would be easy, did you?"

She growled.

He smirked. "Try harder."

She narrowed her eyes and zig-zagged her way toward him. He side-stepped her and took off. Her feet pounded heavily on the ground. "If you want to catch me unaware, you'll have to be much quieter than that. You sound like a heard of buffalo."

Her irritated huff made him laugh. He'd been there—defiant and angry as he learned to use his newly gained powers. Cutting through the hedges, he went still. She ran past, once, twice, and a third time, slower, as she sought him out. Pride rose inside of him. *She's learning fast. We need that.*

On the fourth pass, she hesitated. He sprang from his space, starling her. She stumbled back, before giving chase. He wound around the maze, hoping a hedge to confuse her. The hedges shook as she attempted to follow him. She came shy of making the leap and landed with a thud on the ground. He poked his head through the maze. "Close, but not good enough."

She grunted from her position on her ass. "I'm going to enjoy taking that flag from you."

"If I reach the center of the maze first, I win." He winked before he raced off. He'd had enough of this game. It was past time they began training.

Sitting on the edge of the fountain, he crossed his legs and draped the flag over it. She appeared moments later, breathing heavily. Face flushed, and chest heaving, she glared at him from her bowed position. Hands on her thighs she fought to catch her breath.

"This is an important lesson. If you can't outmatch them in power, outsmart them. You're already going to be at a disadvantage. You're frail, slower, and weaker than the things that will hunt you."

"W-way to deliver a pep talk, c-coach," she wheezed.

"My job is to keep you alive and prepare you for what's to come. I won't stroke your ego, or mince words. This is what we're working with. You have talents they don't, but going toe-to-toe is always going to be a last resort. You need to think faster and work smarter. Use everything around you to your advantage. Tell me how you could've approached this with a different strategy."

"You're faster than me and you know this maze like the back of your hand."

"Yes." He nodded. The answer was obvious to him.

"I could've tried to distract you, maybe."

"That would have been an excellent way to use your powers to your advantage without exhausting yourself. There's a better answer, however."

"Then why don't you tell me." She cocked her hip.

"Because the training is for you."

A wicked smile lined her lips. "Well, I have an idea, but I'd need to test it out."

"What?" he asked, wary of her sudden switch in demeanor.

"I could create a weapon made from nature."

"This weapon would hinder me how?"

She held out her palm. A sphere of crackling yellow energy began to form. "This is concentrated sunlight." She let the ball grow. When it was the size of her head, she stopped. His skin itched, and he stepped back. "Does it work?"

"Yes," he said through his clenched teeth. It wouldn't be long before his skin blistered.

She let the ball wink out.

"Well done. Still not the simplest solution." He shook his head. "What are your resources?"

"Powers."

"And?" He tilted his head.

"Vamp speed?"

"And?" He nudged their link.

"The link," she said softly.

"Everything I know, you potentially know. We need to get used to this. It's a powerful asset, we need to exploit.

"Lessons will be more than physical." He stood. "Are you ready?"

"Do I have a choice?"

"No." Smirking, he shoved her lightly and darted three yards away. "Are you going to take that?" He crossed in front of her and ran in circles around her. She spun, weaving once she got dizzy. Planting her feet, she took a deep breath and held out her hands. Her head popped up and she tracked him. She narrowed her eyes. Her eyes turned purple and she took after him at an impressive clip. He turned, and crouched down, shoulder out. She skidded to a halt, digging her heels into the dirt.

"Better." She shot forward and he flicked her ear and chuckled. "But nowhere near where you need to be." Leaping up from the ground, he ran across the hedges.

"You cheating bastard," she cried. The shrubbery rustled as she followed below him.

He admired her grit. She didn't give up. *Even if she's losing.* He sailed over her head and raced to the entrance. Landing on his feet, he glanced up to see her stumbling out of the archway.

"How did you track me?"

"The bond. It's like having a Crewe GPS."

"Nicely done, Keeta. Now that the games are over, the hard part begins."

"Wait? The hard part?" He walked back toward the castle and she ran up beside him. "Do you consider this easy?"

"That was for your brain. The next step will be for your body."

"From anyone else that would be a come on."

"I'm going to train you until muscle memory takes over, and you can use your brain. You'll be able to wield a sword, fight hand-to-hand, and use your magic. We have to figure out what you can do."

"Oh that's all. No problem."

Ignoring her sarcasm, he continued. "During our downtime, we will search for more information on the spell, and how to repair it."

"Oh, in all our spare time?"

"You got plans for anything else?" He stopped in front of a room and opened the door to reveal a large space lined with padded mats, faded tapestries, and crests from long ago. Weapons lined the walls, carefully placed in holders. He bypassed the spears, crossbows, and maces to heft a sword. The cold steel fit into his palm perfectly. Years of battle and handling had turned Reaver into an extra appendage.

"This is Reaver. He's my oldest possession and dearest friend. He's been with me through thick and thin, and saved my life and others more times than I can guess. He's a longsword. You should always treat your weapon with respect. It will become an extension of who you are."

"Is that why you named it?"

"It was thought to give it power. The first thing I want to do is find a sword that fits your hand and then I'll show you the basics." He spun the swords, warming up as he re-acclimated with Reaver.

"Do I get to name mine?"

"When you bond with her or him, you'll know." He set Reaver aside and led her to the row of swords. She lifted the broadsword with ease, mimicking his hold. With her hair woven into a thick braid, she looked like a warrior woman in training. The vision stirred his desire. Strong and beautiful, she was a woman worthy of a durable mate. The thought of her with anyone else made him snarl.

She froze. "Am I doing something wrong?"

Shaking his head to clear it, he stepped closer. "No."

*You did everything right. It's going to be a problem.*

# Chapter Six

### Keeta

"Call me Belle and dress me in a yellow dress." Her eyes bulged as she stepped into the masculine space. Dark wood lined the two-story room full of books. Shelves were built into the walls, and there was a circular staircase. The center of the room was blocked off by wooden half walls that surrounded the perimeter of the bookshelves. There were more books than one human could read in a lifetime. *I guess vampires don't have that issue though.*

"Who's Belle?" Crewe asked.

"Oh, beastly one, your lack of pop culture knowledge leaves much to be desired." She clucked her tongue as she walked over to the wall and ran her hand over the wood. *How much history does this place house?* A large, ornate table with matching chairs with red velvet cushions sat in the middle of the room. The decadent touches screamed wealth and power. There was a natural accumulation of money that came with living for so long. Logically she understood it, but seeing it in person blew her mind. As an antique lover, she was like a kid in the playground.

"We've spent years gathering everything we could about the spell, and your family. It's a mix of lore, historical documents, and spells." He walked over to the right side. "This section, top and bottom floor, are dedicated exclusively to it."

"I don't know where to start."

"I think it'd be best if you explored on your own. The books may react differently to you."

She nodded. Witches had plenty of tricks to conceal things. Magic attracted magic, and if things were made for her line, no one else would notice anything special. He moved to sit at the table and she opened the gate. The feel of potent magic rushed up to greet her like an eager puppy. These books had been waiting a long time to be found by someone who could use them. Her fingers touched the leather spines and her body began to tingle. They sang a siren call, luring her in. She couldn't quite make out the lyrics, but they were compelling nonetheless.

Closing her eyes, she basked in the magical feedback loop created inside of her. Like a flower after a week of overcast skies, she soaked in the magic. The witches who created this might be long gone, but their spirit and signature energy remained. She pulled a thick, black book off of the shelf. The silver buckles on the corner were patinated, but the spiderweb-esque embellishment was still visible. Two heavy latches with the same designs kept the book shut. Clutching it to her chest, she continued to walk the perimeter. They all sang to her in a different way, but this one demanded to be read first.

Exiting the area, she made her way up the stairwell. It was like being amongst family. It restored her need for familiarity, and the kind of restoration that only came from being in the company of other magic wielders.

*The answer is here.* Her gut and her guides spoke to her. The voice was so clear, she turned to the left, expecting to see a spirit.

"Anything?" Crewe asked.

"Yes. The answer is here. I'm going to start with this one."

She returned to the table and set the heavy book down gingerly. There were years of magic and knowledge in these pages. Brushing her fingers down the latches, she unlocked the hinges and opened the cover. Mardella Creighton had written her name in loopy writing. The year was 1738, and this was her first grimoire as an adult. As she read the other witch's beliefs, she felt connected. She flipped through the pages carefully. Her eyes quickly scanned the writing. The boost from the vampire blood made the research go faster. She paused. *Curse of Imbalance.*

"I think I found something."

"What?" He moved to look over her shoulder. "I don't see anything?" He shook his head.

"That's because you weren't meant to. Let me read it." She cleared her throat, the dust from the book affecting her. "There is talk in the community of the balance between powerful supernatural beings starting to decay. Vampires are rumored to be able to handle more sunlight, and wolves play at changing at will. We believe something occurred to upset the balance. We don't know when, or how to fix it. Research is necessary, but when we must hide, such is impossible."

"So, they knew?" Crewe mumbled.

"It looks like it." She continued to read. "They had more immediate concerns at the time. If they noticed it back then there's a reason why it hasn't gotten this bad until now. There must've been an intervention of sorts." She continued to flip.

"Does it say?"

"No. Most of this is her spells, and family history. There are a few events she felt were important enough to document, but I don't see more about the unbalance yet." She shuddered as she skimmed through the panic that swept through towns looking to blame things they didn't understand on witchcraft. Things weren't perfect in the world, but people were able to live their lives as they saw fit.

"If the books weren't meant for us, why were we able to open them?"

"Because if you open a book and find nothing of interest, you don't continue to search. A locked book screams secrets. We've survived for a long time by remaining hidden. You should relate to that."

"Are you actually complimenting vampires?"

"Drawing a comparison, but if it makes you feel better, sure." She winked.

He ignored her dig, but she could feel the equivalent to an eye roll via their bond. He wasn't the iceman he appeared to be, he just hid his emotions, because heaven forbid he appear too mortal. An electrical surge swept through her body. She twitched as the image of a tiny brown leather book and a map etched onto leather flashed in her head.

The feel of room temperature hands on her shoulders pulled her back to the present. She winced as her head pounded.

"What happened?" Crewe's voice dripped concern.

"I think I had a vision. I saw a strange map and a small leather book." She struggled to remember the details as the images faded.

"Close your eyes and relax. Why was the map strange?"

"It was burned into a supple brown leather, and it felt odd."

"Tell me why it was odd." His voice was soft and soothing. She felt safe with him there.

"It felt powerful. No ... Magical." She opened her eyes. "A magical map?"

"Is it any stranger than the rest of what we've experienced?"

"Fair point." Her shoulders slumped as a wave of exhaustion swept over her.

"Nakeeta?"

"I'm okay. Visions take a lot." Closing her eyes, she rubbed her lids.

"Let's take a break and get something to eat." He squeezed her shoulder.

"No, we don't have time for breaks." She pushed him away. There'd be no pitying the human who couldn't keep up.

"And what do you plan on doing like this?" He gestured with his hands.

"I'm going to figure the vision out. I'm more than a vessel people can use to convey things. I'm going to do it on my own terms." She rose. "I'm inducing a true vision."

"Now?"

"It's all about our main goal, remember?"

His jaw clenched. "We've moved past that."

"Since when?"

"I can feel how tired you are. I didn't take you for reckless."

"And I didn't think you'd become my nursemaid." The inability to control her life compounded, setting her off like a firecracker on the Fourth of July.

"I'm not the reason you're upset."

"Now you're an expert on all things Keeta?"

"You know you can't hide your real feelings from me."

Grabbing the wall between them, she slammed it down, imagining thick-paned steel surrounded by barbwire.

"I'm almost impressed." He toppled the wall over with a light push of his own mental strength. "Should I treat you like I do my men when they get insubordinate?"

"I'd like to see you try." She balled her fists.

"You require a different tactic."

She tensed, preparing herself for his next move. He pinned her into the chair, gripping the wooden arms on either side. "You need a firm hand. I can respect an independent woman. You've been on your own for a long time. However, this is over your head. If you burn out now, what chance do we have?" He leaned in and she shrank down in her seat, attempting to avoid his pene-trating gaze and all-consuming presence. "I tried to keep this strictly business. But you insisted on cracking open my shell and climbing inside. Now you get to deal with the monster I try to kept leashed."

She swallowed and he glanced down at the muscles working in her neck. "My bond says you're mine. Much like a sire, I feel responsibility and an emo-tional attachment. It's been a long time since I felt that. When you endanger yourself, you agitate the beast. You saw what he's capable of in my past. If you threaten your own safety, I'll be forced to take drastic measures."

Her heartbeat kicked up a notch.

"Do you want to find out what that means?"

"I won't be frightened." She tilted her chin, refusing to cower before him.

"What he'll do won't be scary." He gave her a sinful grin that curled her toes and excited her more than it frightened her.

She licked her lips and stopped. *Do I want to know what he means by this?* The dark glimmer in his eyes and the smirk were a silent challenge. *I haven't backed down yet.*

"Prove it."

His eyes flashed red and he moved a millimeter from her lips. "Be sure. I do nothing lightly."

"Now who's hesitating?" she asked breathily.

His lips touched hers lightly, the barest hint of a butterfly's wing. He held her gaze, as they grazed hers again; longer, harder. Gripping his soft Henley shirt, she let him take the lead. He buried his fingers in her hair, massaging her scalp, and traced her lips with the tip of his tongue. She opened her mouth on a moan, and hummed as the taste of strawberries flooded her senses. Kissing Crewe was an entirely new experience.

The essence of who he was flavored his clever tongue and skillful lips. The pleasure he felt was broadcasted across their link, doubling her enjoyment. He tilted his head, and she mirrored the movement as they both sought out more contact. Their tongues were caught up in a carefully choreographed dance as they tangled, caressed, and at times battled for dominance. Her body tingled, and her stomach muscles tightened. Pulling away, she sucked in a shaky breath, and he rested his lips against her forehead.

Her mind had been blown with a simple kiss. An avalanche of emotions barreled toward her. "Crewe?" Her voice sounded fearful.

"It's okay." He closed the link between them.

"How can you feel all of that?" she asked, stunned.

"*Everything* is amplified for us. It's why we have to keep such a tight rein on ourselves. This is why I asked if you were sure. There's no easily flipped off switch."

"I didn't understand." The weight of responsibility threatened to crush her.

"Are you regretting it so soon, flower?" His lips curled up into a sad smile.

The nickname melted away the apprehension. "I'm just trying to understand."

"We'll learn together. This is new to me, too. Vampires don't have mates. Much like humans, we have a choice and free will."

"And you chose me?" she said, humbled.

"There was no other choice." He stood. "Enough. Now we eat."

"The spell—"

"Can wait."

Slightly dazed from the strange turn of events, she acquiesced.

## CREWE

*Sard.* He was tightrope walking without a net. Worse, he was fool enough to think it might be worth it. Peering across the table to the woman eating her steak, salad, and baked potato with gusto, he felt his spirit lift for the first time in centuries. Always, he'd been dedicated to his men, Dregan, and the mission. *She* was new and dangerous territory. A weakness he couldn't afford. The bond had been a slippery slope he continued to ride straight down. He'd never been this close to another person. The connection they shared differed from any he'd ever encountered. The one he held with Dregan came the closest. He felt deeply for the man who'd saved him from insanity and death.

Colors were brighter. He stared at the stained glass he'd seen a million times or more. The emerald scales on the dragon contrasted with the blue spines on his back, around his facial area, and the reds and oranges of his mouth and forked tongue. The wooden table was polished to a high shine. He could smell the lingering lemony scent from the cleaning crew they brought in monthly. She'd disrupted the monotony and woke him from an extended sleep.

"It's weird eating while you sit there."

"I'm having my lunch as well." He lifted his goblet. "It's just liquid."

"Can you eat?"

He grimaced. "If I have to. It does nothing for me. My body doesn't break it down like yours. We sweat the unnecessary things out in blood."

"No going out to eat. Got it."

"You make light of these things?" He'd spent so long hiding the things that made him different, her easy acceptance felt wrong.

"Dude. I have purple eyes when I get angry, I crave blood, and we don't know what the hell else I might start doing at some point. I can't throw stones when I live in a glass house. Besides, aren't we trying to build a better world? Saving the shitty one seems a little pointless unless we're trying to do better. That means bringing our people together."

"You ask for too much."

"No, I ask for what we should've already done to be started."

He shook his head. "Not everyone will take kindly to that point of view. My people are slow to change—"

"And look where that's gotten them. If I'm the savior of the world, I should have some say in things."

"You can speak out all you want. It doesn't mean they'll listen. The approach has to be particular." Most of the vampires in charge were old school. An opinionated slip of a woman who was a witch to boot? Her words would automatically fall on deaf ears.

"So, they expect me to help them, risk my life, and then … what, remain silent? Bow down like a servant? Slavery and the oppression of women are both over." Her eyes flashed purple and her full lips puckered. The fire inside of her shone bright. He was drawn to the light she gave off like a bonfire. Her passion and spirit attracted him like a bee to honey. There was an intrinsic sweetness that dripped from her pores, and he wanted to sample every drop. She was life after centuries of death.

"I can't speak for all of them, but know you'll be facing an uphill battle."

"Will I face it alone?"

Could he turn his back on his people after a lifetime spent serving them? The ring of his phone broke the peace.

"I'll be right back." He moved quickly to answer it. He was unsurprised to see Dreagan's number.

"Hello."

"Have you found the answer?" Dregan asked. The lack of pleasantries told him his boss was feeling the pressure. If nothing, Dregan preferred to keep things civilized.

"Not yet. She had a vision today. A breakthrough maybe. We know what we're looking for. The books we've gathered react differently to her."

"Differently how?" Dregan asked.

"She sees things in them we never could. I watched her read from what appeared to be a blank page."

Dregan gave a humorless laugh. "Clever witches. I need more." The sadness in his tone seeped over the airwaves.

"What's happened?" Crewe braced himself for impact. The loses they'd suffered recently were severe casualties.

"We had an unexpected situation among the old ones. We put him to ground in hopes he'll recover later, once we've found a cure and set things to right. We had to put down his inner circle. They attacked once he did."

Crewe bowed his head and rubbed his eye. "Who?" They couldn't afford to lose old ones.

"I told you, an old one and his personal coven."

"*Dregan* ..." He put the emphasis in his tone. He was trying to keep things from him.

"Kazimir."

"Kaz?" His voice shook. The arrogant, impeccably dressed, and light-hearted vampire had been one of the first to welcome him into their life. As a child of Dregan who he'd pledged himself to with a blood oath, they were family in a way. The same blood ran through their veins.

"It was the same illness?" Crewe asked.

"Yes. It's like they've lost their ability to know when it's time to go to ground, and it's leading them to go past the point of no return."

"Perhaps they are. The book mentioned the decline of the spell as far back as the early eighteen hundreds. Keeta believes they must've taken some preventive measure to keep things from falling apart until now."

"Interesting theory. How is she adapting?"

"Better than we could've anticipated. Between researching we train."

"Is she ready?"

"No, but she will be."

"I will arrive soon for a visit." If his heart still beat, it'd be racing. "I want to see who we'll be putting all of our trust in."

"We'll be expecting you." He heard the words that went unsaid. If Dregan wasn't impressed with what he saw, there'd be hell to pay. Their time was running out faster than either had anticipated.

Retracing his steps, he formed a plan.

"What happened?"

"That was Dregan. He'll be visiting us soon."

"That's bad, isn't it?"

"It depends on the progress we made," he answered carefully.

"You want me to do that spell now?" She pushed her plate away.

Folding his hands behind his back, he opened his mouth to eat a healthy helping of crow. "Yes, I believe it would be prudent."

She smirked. "I love it when you speak the Queen's English."

"It's the proper English. You Yankees have desecrated it." He shook his head

"Oh, is a certain vampire expressing pride for his across the pond status?"

"We were here first, darling. You left and came over here to escape us, but it doesn't make you less a part of us when you boil it all down."

"Touché, Brit."

Only this woman would be bold enough to tease him.

"I've ended people for such blatant shows of disrespect. You know that, right?"

She arched an eyebrow. "But I'm not most people, am I?"

"No, you're not. I'm still deciding if that's a good thing."

"You and me both." She sighed. "I need a few things for the spell."

"We have an apothecary's worth of herbs available." Her eyes lit up and he chuckled. "Such a sassy little witch."

A CONCOCTION OF OIL, MARIGOLD, rosemary, clove, mugwort, lavender, jasmine, and rose later, Keeta was in heaven. She ground the mixture up with a mortar and pestle, releasing the fragrant scent of the freshly dried herbs. The sweet and savory blended together to form a pleasant aroma. Sage burned in an abalone shell. It was one thing to know how things worked, and another to see them being used. Her warm honey brown skin glowed with a power that made her appear ethereal.

Loose, her curls tumbled around her body as she hummed. It was easy to envision a witch of old working in the small stone enclosure they'd turned into a witch's kitchen. A hearth stood across the room and shelves were lined with herbs, salts, pots, and equipment. He'd never worked closely with a witch, though there were free-lance practitioners who would do a spell for the right price. Dregan took care of those and oversaw the stocking of this space.

Life had been about orders and responsibilities before. Now, he wondered about the witch. How did Dregan know her? They worked together on numerous occasions. Why did they have so much tolerance for one another? It shamed him to realize he'd become a robot. He did what he was ordered, asked no questions, and put no thought into things. He'd fallen into a rut where living stopped and existing began.

"Okay. All done."

"Now what?"

"You can leave, or sit still and silent like a statue while I anoint myself with oil and go into a trance."

"I'm not going anywhere."

"I figured as much." She sighed. "Going into a trance can be dangerous if I'm distracted, and it's going to be harder with you here. It requires total relaxation and vulnerability. If you stay you need to be mindful of your emotions and our connections. You don't need to shut the link down, but you need to limit it."

He gave a curt nod, ignoring the spark of irritation that tried to catch at the self-imposed distance. He moved to sit across from her against the wall, as she sat on a pile of pillows, crossed her legs, and rested her hands lightly on her knees. Closing her eyes, she inhaled and exhaled. Calm swept through the room. His chest rose and feel, synching to her as he sank into a meditative state of his own.

He retreated into the parts of his mind he rarely visited. The center of his brain was a peaceful oasis. A lush green area, shaded perfectly by an overcast sky, and a crisp, windy day with a light drizzle. It was the weather he'd grown up with. The scent of freshly baked pies drifted to where he sat on a stone bench.

"Crewe." He glanced up, stunned by the appearance of Kazimir. Mental conversation wasn't unusual between those of the same bloodline, but it was incredibly rare because they rarely let their guard down this way.

"Are you really here?"

"Yes. It's easier to use the energy I have when I'm in the ground this way."

"What happened?"

"What happened was planned. It was a sacrifice I was willing to make for the greater good. The only future where we survive is one that sees witches and vampires united. When the spell was damaged it acted like a poison injected into all of us. Slowly over the years it's caused more aggression, darkness, and now the final death rattle of insanity. You have to be very careful who you trust. Minds are being warped by this invasion and people aren't who they once were."

"You believe we have a traitor in our midst?"

"Yes."

"And why do you know so much?"

"About a year ago, I was approached by a coven of witches."

"And they lived?" Crewe asked, stunned.

"They outnumbered me. They were powerful, and only looking to talk. I knew it'd be easier to hear them out than it would be to fight. The things they told me rang true, and the rest terrified me. It takes a lot to do that."

"What did they say?"

"They saw the end for all of us if we didn't work together. They knew about the search. Things from before my time as a vampire that no one else knew. So, when they told me what would happen if we don't succeed, I believed them."

"Why did they come to you?"

"They saw that my future was connected to them. They're the reason I'm still rational and able to talk to you."

"Why can't we do this for all of us?" Crewe asked. The thought of a temporary cure was exciting.

"It took the entire coven to do this, and it's been draining. It wouldn't be a solution." He shook his head. "Not to mention, they'd have to trust the witches enough to let them close, and we both know we're a long way away from that. Your girl will be able to help."

"You know about Keeta?"

Kaz nodded. "She was also in their visions."

The thought concerned him. He bristled. He didn't know these people.

"They're on her side. None of us would ever endanger her. She's the light in these dark times. Come and find the coven. I'm weakening and there's still much left to explain."

"Where are you?"

"Savannah, Georgia. The spells have been laid. They'll find you when you arrive."

"I'm not sure that's reassuring, Kaz."

"I have to go. Remember what I said. Savannah, Georgia." Kaz said.

"Got it."

"Come soon." He faded away, and Crewe was pulled from his peaceful place. He blinked and found Keeta kneeling before him.

"Crewe?"

"I'm here."

She sat back on her heels. "Where did you go?"

"To visit with a friend." He focused on her features. "Are you okay?"

"Yes. We have a lot of work to do and not much time." Overwhelmed, she tugged on her on her braid.

"Who told you that?"

"My great-grandmother. I don't think I would've listened to anyone else." Bashfully, she rubbed the back of neck.

Apprehension slithered down their bond.

"What did she say, Nakeeta?"

"We need to strengthen our bond."

"Is that what you're worried about?" He cupped her chin. "That is already happening. What's wrong?"

"We need to drink from one another." She peered down, hiding behind her long, dark lashes.

"Blood exchanges will make everything go faster." Picking at her shirt, she avoided his gaze.

She struggled with the urge to fidget. "There may be side effects."

"Is that what you're worried about?" he asked.

She lifted her gaze to meet his blue eyes. "Aren't you?"

His eyes were kind and softer than they'd been when they first meet. The man had changed so much during their time together. *And maybe I have, too.* "We choose who we connect to. I've already made my decision. Nothing you can do will alter that. This may accelerate things, but it won't take away my choice." That someone could care about his rights floored him. This woman had a big heart. How could he not want her? The purity that radiated off her made him feel clean, like he could one day be worthy of the gift her affection and devotion would be. He stroked his thumb down the side of her neck, circling her pulse point.

Her breathing increased. "You barely know me."

"It is only with the heart one can see rightly," he quoted a line from *The Little Prince.*

"*The Little Prince?*"

He nodded. "Until you I had begun to doubt I still possessed the organ. There was never another option."

Her faced heated. He ran his thumb down her high cheekbone, chasing the warmth.

"Crewe." Her lips trembled.

"I'm not looking for anything more than what you're ready to give. I'm a man who has nothing but time, and you're a woman worth waiting a lifetime for. I'd say we're perfectly matched."

Her lips twitched upward. "Well when you put it like that …"

"What else did she say?"

"Because that wasn't enough? Are you trying to tempt fate?"

"No, I'm reading your emotions through the bond."

"If we wanted to survive this we needed to lean on each other and be careful who we trust."

He nodded thoughtfully. "Yes, Kaz said much the same. He wanted us to meet a coven of vampire and witches who want to help us."

"Where?"

"Savannah, Georgia."

"Well that'll be simple then. Do you trust him?"

"Kaz? I want to."

"But you still feel uncertain?" Cocking her head to the side, she studied him.

He cupped her face in his hands. "I will never take unnecessary risks when it comes to you."

"Because I'm the chosen one, right? Just call me Keeta Potter."

"I think we both know it's beyond that." He skimmed his lips over hers. She fisted his shirt, and pressed her lips toward his, slipping her tongue between his parted lips. The initiation lit a spark inside of him. He pulled her onto his lap and tilted his head as he devoured her full lips. She tasted like grapefruit with sprinkles of sugar. He fed on her lips, sucking down the goodness and hope she offered.

Allowing himself to feel, he placed his duty on the back burner, and drowned in the emotions she brought forth. She wrapped her arms and legs around him, surrounding him in her scent and with her caring. Like a staved man, he took it all in and held it close. Storing the memory in to his heart. Their link hummed between them and for a moment he swore he felt his heart beat again.

# Chapter Seven

### Keeta

FEET BRACED, SHE HELD THE sword at shoulder level, and stepped toward Crewe and to the right to avoid his attack as he taught her. His sword came down. They clashed in a clank of metal.

"Good." He countered, stepping forward and bringing his blade down. She leaned back and off center, dodging the blow. Lowering her sword, she kept him from taking another swipe. He allowed her to use steady pressure to control his use of the blade.

"Excellent." They found a rhythm and he increased his speed little by little. She did her best to keep up as he pushed her limits. Ignoring the burn in her arms she continued to block, and wait for her moment to thrust. His sword came down, faster than she could block, and bit into her shoulder. The pads took the brunt of the blow, but she stumbled back regardless.

"I'm calling it for the day." Sweat dripped from every pore. Her heart thudded in her chest, and her limbs were shaky from overuse. Hours spent pushing herself to the brink physically and emotionally as she accessed his muscle memory and training were finally taking its toll. Frustrated, she held her sword, blade facing down. Every day an invisible clock continued its relentless countdown and she never felt close enough to the goal. She'd never shot a gun or wielded a weapon in her knife, and now she was training like a Navy Seal preparing to go into a mission.

"I can do more."

"We have plenty of other things to occupy us," he reminded her gently. They'd yet to find a lead for the map or the worn notebook she'd seen in her vision. Everything she'd read since in the library had been helpful, but unrelated to their mission. She felt like she was missing a piece of the puzzle. Why show her that on the first day, only to remain elusive? "We will break to refresh ourselves, eat lunch, and retire to the library for the evening."

Lunch meant more than food. It meant an exchange of blood. Her stomach flipped and her mouth watered. The hunger rose inside of her, eager to be satiated. She raked her eyes over his fit form. The feeding had taken on a sensual tone. Licking her lips, she imagined the taste of strawberries filling her mouth as the thick blood coated her throat and gave her strength. There was an intimacy in being nourished by another person.

"Sounds like a plan."

"Your eyes are purple." His eyes flashed red in return.

"I'm parched."

"A gentleman never makes a lady wait." He removed his neck guard. She stepped forward, hypnotized by the expanse of flesh he'd revealed. Tilting his head to the left, he cupped her head and pulled her toward him. She nuzzled his neck, inhaling his scent like a cat. Sucking his skin into her mouth, she groaned as his sweetness bled through the pores.

"You ready?"

She released his skin with a pop. "Yes."

He lengthened his nail and slashed his neck. The scent of blood sent her into a frenzy and she latched on, moaning as the liquid trickled into her mouth.

A split second later his teeth sank into her neck. Her body shuddered as pleasure rolled through it. Her knees weakened, and she leaned on him heavily. He pressed her closer and they pulled the blood out in tandem. Pushing her thighs together, she tried to relieve the pressure building. Her flesh prickled with awareness, and her body tingled. She wrestled down the urge to rock against him. Prying her lips away, she breathed heavily as she watched him through lowered lids.

The ruby eyes that once frightened her, now held their own beauty. She traced their deep-set shape, marveling at the ability to explore the powerful being holding her in his arms. He licked the leftover blood from her lips and she moaned. "Crewe."

"What do you want, Keeta?"

"You."

He lapped at her neck, sealing his bite marks. "Then you'll have me."

When he lifted her in his arms, she wound her legs around him. "I need a shower."

"Let me take care of that." He captured her lips and she lost herself to his clever tongue, trusting him to get her to the room safely. Trailing her fingernails over his scalp, she bit his bottom lip. He shuddered, and she rejoiced in the brief control she had over him. Nipping and sucking her way down his neck, she teased him relentlessly. The whoosh of air around her made her laugh as he used vamp speed. They stopped at his door.

"Are you sure—"

Her lips pressed against his was the only answer she could manage around the lump that formed in her throat. It'd been a long time since she'd had physical contact with a man. Between working to fulfill her dreams, and healing from psychic annihilation, she'd been busy and in no shape to be that vulnerable with anyone. Unlocking the door, he slipped inside.

"Wait here, while I prepare everything?"

She nodded and slid down his body meekly before landing on her own feet.

"What's wrong, love? You nervous?"

"I've never had anyone treat me like this."

He scowled darkly. "You deserve nothing less. I'll make you forget all of the boys who came before me. Knight's promise." His words made her quiver as he moved through the door that housed a modernized bathroom. Sinking down on a chair, she placed her hands in her lap and waited, clearing her mind.

"You're thinking too much."

She glanced up at Crewe and smiled. He could no longer sneak up on her. "That means I'm not doing my job well." Kneeling in front of her, he untied her sneakers and pulled off her socks. His hands skimmed over her muscles as he stripped her clothing off one article at a time. She stood before him in nothing more than a black sports bra and matching boy shorts.

"You're more beautiful than I imagined." His fingertips skimmed over her belly and her muscles twitched in response. "Hold that thought." He placed a gentle kiss on her forehead and flashed away, returning with a small sweet smile that melted her internally into a puddle. Holding out his hand, he guided her into the bathroom. Candles flickered on the marble counter, and mounds of bubbles floated on top of the claw-footed bathtub.

"You did all of this for me? I'm shocked you had it laying around."

"Baths were a luxury in my time. The water was often tepid, and soaps were handmade and harsh. I indulge in toiletries now and candlelight makes me remember my time." The more he opened up, the more attractive he became.

"I feel underdressed." She bit her bottom lip as guilt swept over her. What was he getting out of this?

Framing her face with his hands, he rested his forehead against hers. "I've never had a woman who mattered before. My life was harsh and unpredictable. I knew I'd never take a wife or carry on my name. Being with you like this is more than I ever let myself hope for. You please me by allowing me the honor of being intimate with you."

*How can he be real?* Once she peeled back his layers, she'd discovered a priceless treasure.

"You're mine. I plan to worship every inch of you." He ran his finger along the edge of her bra, sending goosebumps over her flesh. "Lift your arms." She obeyed, only breaking their gaze when the fabric obscured her vision. Hooking his thumbs into her underwear, he rolled them down, and helped her out of them and toward the tub.

She stepped over the sides and sank into the blissfully warm water that smelled of lavender. Resting her head against the edge of the tub, she studied him as he grabbed a flannel and lathered a bar of thick handmade soap. He grabbed her hand, gently washing her skin with a focused attention that made her feel like a queen. The enormity of things they had to accomplish was forgotten. She clung to the joy bubbling up inside of her.

Clean, she sat up and crooked her finger. "Come here." He leaned in and she captured his bottom lip, biting down hard enough to draw blood. He groaned as she drank from his wound. Moving back, she licked the last drops as he healed.

"It's awfully lonely, and you're overdressed."

"Impatient, are we?"

She nodded her head, drinking him in as he quickly removed his clothing. Muscles flexed under pale skin. He moved like a large cat, stalking its prey. His eyes flickered from red to blue as he joined her.

"Come here." His voice dropped an octave as he pulled her to sit on his lap, his legs on either side of her body.

"I don't get to clean you?"

"There's no point. The rest of my plans involve getting filthy." He rolled his hips and she gasped. Their wet bodies slid together. She arched her back and lost herself to the seductive spell they were weaving as they joined more than their spirits.

THE CRACK OF THUNDER, PRECEDED by a bright flash of lightning, drew her attention from the words that swam on the yellowed pages in front of her. Her skin prickled. Hairs begin to rise, and she shifted in her seat. "This storm is wrong," she whispered. There was power building up behind the weather, or perhaps causing it.

She stood and walked from the table, pressing her nose to the cold glass like a child. "Who knows we're here?" Nervous energy added to her anxiety. Clouds raced over the sky, blocking out the full moon. A slash of lightning exploded, turning the clouds an eerie neon green. Swirling fog crept over the grounds.

"Wrong in what way?" Crewe joined her to watch the abnormal display.

"It's unnatural. Can't you feel it?" She opened their link, letting her emotions bleed into his.

He tensed. "Are we under attack?"

"I'm not sure." The words felt like a lie. People didn't work this kind of magic for shits and giggles.

"I'm not taking a chance. Let's get to a more secure location."

She smiled sadly. "There's no place you can hide from magic. It's specific like that. Standing your ground, and hoping you have enough magic to equal or overpower the other person is all you have. Focus. This is no novice." Lightning struck the ground close to the castle. She twitched. It struck again closer, turning up the ground. A wind tunnel began to form, the base as dark as night.

"They're calling me out."

"Who?"

The evil feeling of black magic crawled up her spine. She knew the signature well.

"Genevieve. The Priestess."

"Can you defeat her?"

"Before? No. Now." She shrugged. "It's hard to say. Why is she looking for me?"

"She must know who you truly are."

She rubbed her arms to counter the chill setting in. "If she did, she never would've let me go."

"How did you escape her the first time?"

She bowed her head. "I found a suitable replacement. I seduced a witch with latent powers, gave her a place to belong, and showed her all of the pretty things that came along with the coven. Once she was hooked, I was freed." Her throat swelled. "I'm not proud of what I did—"

"But we all do what we must to survive."

Saline blurred her vision as she nodded. A boom went off directly above the house. The rumble seemed to shake the ground.

"She won't stop."

"You can't mean to go out there."

"I have to." Her gut pulled her toward the front door. She turned, and the hem of her deep pink dress skimmed her toes. Better to remain barefoot, so she could tap into the earth's energy. Unlike years before, she felt no fear. Calm descended over her as she made the long trek through the castle at a leisurely pace. *Let her wait. She no longer owns you.* The voice inside enhanced her confidence and helped snap the lingering chains that held her tight to the way things once were. Once you'd given your submission to a person, it was hard as hell to take it back completely.

Crewe trailed behind her, brooding and apprehensive. It wasn't in his blood to remain on the sidelines. He wanted to be in the thick of it, defending her. Her heart swelled. They reached the front door, and she turned to face him. Placing her hands on his chest, she looked up. "I know you'll want to help, but this fight is mine."

"If you're hurt—"

"All I'm asking you to do is be backup. Not the front line."

His jaw clenched, and he nodded. He brought his hand up to his wrist, sank his fangs in, and then brought it to her lips. "Drink."

She latched on to the sweet nectar and sucked it down in greedy mouthfuls.

His power charged her like a battery. The wound healed and she pulled back, licking her lips. Centering herself, she used her power to push the heavy door open and stepped into the howling winds, head held high. Her feet padded along the wet stone as she moved toward the grassy knoll where a figure stood in a black dress, shrouded by darkness. She knew all of the intimidation tactics, so she dismissed them. Genevie might be using the same old tricks, but she had a new bag of them to unleash.

Shield lifted, she flinched at the lightning strikes raining down on either side of her. The ground shook under the onslaught. She stumbled as the earth rocked, but never fell. Using her newly gained speed, would be giving away her hand. For now, she'd play the role to gather as much information as possible. Genevie threw back her hood and scowled. Her slender, oval-shaped face was every bit as flawless as she remembered. No wrinkle dare mar her forehead or around her deepest black eyes. Full lips painted black turned down. Her eyebrows drew together as she looked at her with disgust.

"What do you want, Genevie? Our business was concluded long ago."

"And yet, I hear you of all the beings on this planet are the key to a revolution. I knew I shouldn't have let you go. Of course, once I have your blood, there's nowhere you could hide that I wouldn't find you."

"Here I stand in plain sight." Keeta held up her arms.

"Do you think your vampire will help you?"

She smirked. "I don't need him."

Genevie blinked. "Bold. Have you forgotten who I am?"

"No. I've discovered who I am."

"This is our chance to rule. The vampires are unstable. Soon the wolves will turn on one another to determine pack hierarchy. It's the opening we've been waiting for. Humans will be the ones to hide in the shadows."

"And you think witches, who mostly strive to keep the balance, will be on board for this? The darkness needs the light to exist. What do you suppose would happen if you removed one?"

"Always a bleeding heart. It's why you never lasted. All of that power wasted on ideology."

"Morals and compassion," Keeta disputed.

"Weakness spelled by another name has the same meaning. I'm here to take you back. You're a hot commodity."

"Then we've reached an impasse because I'm not going anywhere with you."

Throwing back her head, Genevie laughed. "I was hoping you'd say that." She lifted her hand and brought it down in a sweeping motion. Lightning struck the place Keeta once stood.

"What sorcery is this?" Genevie hissed.

"Didn't they tell you I was different?" She continued to dodge the lightning strikes as she wove her way through the trees that lined the property and searched for others. Genevie rarely played fair.

"Not so different I see. You're still running." The smell of another witch came from inside of the maze. *Got you.* She dug her heels into the perimeter of the maze, making a small trench. Infusing the lines with her power, she began to mouth a spell. "I bind you from doing harm. I call on the archetypal energy." The hedge rustled. A tall, thin witch with thick chestnut-colored hair and a heart-shaped face twisted into a feral expression greeted her.

"Harper." Seeing the dark aura surrounding the once sweet girl opened the wound.

"I've been waiting a long time for this moment," Harper whispered.

"I'm sorry."

A blast of energy nailed Keeta in the back. She flew into the air, landing on the lawn twenty feet away. She coughed, wincing as she struggled to bring air into her lungs. The fog rose up to conceal her body. She gained her knees slowly. Reoriented, she sped away.

"Come and face me, you coward." Harper's shrill cries smacked of insanity. If she took out Genevie, the girl would falter. A clap of thunder followed a rapid-fire lightning display. The rain came down in thick sheets that obscured her vision and threw off the traces of others.

The ground cracked beneath her feet. She teetered on the edge of the rapidly forming chasm. Regaining her balance, she jumped back. Spinning, she saw Genevie a few feet away. Keeta channeled the rain into a waterspout that slammed into the other witch like a concrete wall. She followed the attack with a blast of crackling blue energy.

Shoved to the side by another witch, she pulled the fog up to hide her position as she dodged a blow. Her body went stiff when she was hit by a nasty hex.

"Hold her," Genevie cried.

Throwing her head back, Keeta cracked Harper's nose. A metallic aroma filled the air as she broke free from the bind. Pivoting on her heels, she kicked Harper in the gut. The gloves were off. Softening the dirt, Keeta made a downward motion. Harper screamed as she sank into the marshy ground up to her neck.

"I bind you, Harper Peede, by the blood spilled on the grounds of my property, from causing harm to others in this space. May the ground swallow you whole if you raise a hand." White strands of magic wove around her and disappeared as they sank into her skin. "Next time I'll do more than take your magic temporarily," she snarled.

Pain erupted on her back. She cried out as her skin split, and blood trickled onto the dress.

"Still leaving a blind spot."

She turned, gritting her teeth. "Still sending others to do your dirty work and unable to win a fair fight."

"Do you truly believe you could beat me?" Genevie screamed.

"Let's find out." She sent the energy out of her body in a dark flame. Hitting her knees, she watched as the black flames caught the hem of her dress. Genevie struggled to extinguish the unnatural flames. Pouncing on her distraction. Keeta channeled the fear, anger, and hate she held in her heart for the priestess she slashed down, honing her powers like a sharpened blade. Crimson blood flew as her spell hit. Balling her fists, she infused the priestess with pain. Genevie collapsed.

*Finish her off. Spill her blood.* The beast inside of her wanted carnage. Her senses alerted her moments before she was thrown off her feet by a shoulder to the gut. Pain exploded through her body. She landed in a heap of weakened limbs. There was magic behind that hit. Peering up through her tangled curls, she dug her fingers into the ground as she spotted the male.

"Demarcus." She growled at the suave, black-haired man with a chiseled jaw, broad shoulders, and shoulder-length dreads. He stood in front of his mistress.

"What have you become?"

"Your worst mistake." She leapt at him, letting the beast take control. Her mouth ached as fangs pushed up from her gums and she went for his jugular. Her teeth scraped his flesh as Crewe's nails raked down his side.

"*Get her!*" He moved toward the Priestess. A bright flash of light blinded her. She stumbled back, throwing a hand over her eyes to shield them. A second later, the witches were gone. Spitting his blood onto the ground, she scrubbed her mouth, horrified. Her chest grew tight, and her stomach rebelled. Bending over, she emptied the contents of her belly. Tears spilled down her cheeks.

"What am I?"

He wiped her mouth with his sleeve. "Powerful."

"I'm a freak."

He glanced around. "What's to keep them from returning?"

Sniffling, she drew on the energy generated by the fading storm and wove a complex ward around the property. Dripping the blood from her healing lip onto the ground, she sealed it with her blood.

"Your wards are powerful, but we were blood bound once. It gave them the ability to find me regardless of where I was."

"And now?"

"Now, they can't." Numb, she rocked back and forth, wishing the rain beating down could wash away the confusion clouding her mind.

He reached out for her. "Come. We both need rest."

"How could I sleep after that?"

"The first time you use your fangs is always traumatic."

Brows furrowed, she tossed her hands in the air. "Fangs is what's wrong in this situation, Crewe!"

"Perhaps this is a part of your witch's plan, melding us."

"I could do without being the prototype," she snapped.

"Nakeeta?" He grabbed her wrist, stopping her just inside of the door.

"Yes?"

"You did bloody excellent out there."

She couldn't help but grin at his praise. He didn't give it lightly. "Thank you."

Twining their fingers, he brought their hands up to his lips. It fixed nothing, but it showed her she wasn't alone. With the darkness clawing at her insides, begging to be unleashed, it would have to be enough.

### CREWE

HE SIPPED THE HONEYED MEAD and observed the other knights digging into their food. They were celebrating a victory. That meant a fresh round of baths, wenches, and all of the food they could manage to fit in their bellies. When things were good, they lived like kings. These were the moments he'd left home for.

"I can't believe I'm forced to come back to this wretched time. As if living through it once wasn't enough."

"Peace, sister. This is the easiest way."

The voices stood out amongst the merriment. He turned to see the strange women dressed in long, black gowns. They weren't tavern wenches, and a lady of nobility wouldn't be caught here. Tall and regal with flowing hair the color of spun straw, and night, they studied him.

"He noticed us," the golden-haired beauty said with a welcoming smile.

"Yes. He's stronger than I anticipated," the other said. Her gaunt, oval-shaped face, thin lips, and upturned nose exacerbated the pinched expression she wore.

"It is the bond. Fear not, brave knight. We brought you here in sleep to speak to the male we've entrusted the future with," the blonde said.

This was more than a dream.

"Buried in your memories, we can speak freely without being tracked. I am Angele, and this is Moll."

"What do you want from me?" he asked, suspicious of the witches distorting his memories and entering his mind. The power it took to manage that on one as old as he was vast.

"To see if you are worthy," Moll snarled. Her dark eyes were hostile.

"It appears you've already made up your mind." He leaned back in the cathedral style seat with its high arched back and oversized armrests.

"Brave," Angele conceded.

"Or stupid," Moll said, unimpressed.

"Nakeeta has chosen you, and you have chosen her. Are you willing to do whatever it takes to keep her safe?" Angele asked.

"Yes."

"Even if it means going against your own kind?" Moll questioned further.

"I understand what's at stake."

"Yes, but what are you willing to give to succeed?"

"My life if necessary."

"You vampires, all about death. Never understanding the power to be found in living." Moll shook her head. "What if we require the opposite from you?"

"Then you've come to the wrong creature."

"So quickly you give up," Moll accused.

"Moll." Angele rested a hand on her shoulder. "He is not the enemy."

"So that automatically makes him *the one?*" Shaking her head, Moll jabbed her finger at him.

"You come into my mind and insult me?" He pounded his fist on the table and stood. "Enough with your veiled comments. If you wish to ask something of me, do so. Otherwise, I kindly bid you exit my dreams." His tone was terse, but he chose his words carefully. They were all precariously balanced on a razor's edge. Each needed the other to survive, yet the misunderstandings and mistrust ran deep.

The women exchanged a look. "She doesn't need you to die for her. She needs you to live," Angele whispered.

*Witches and their cryptic messages.*

They stepped toward him, and he took a giant step back, evading their touch.

"Not so stupid," Moll whispered.

"Be still, vampire. We've decided to give you a gift."

"So you claim, yet you've explained nothing."

"We can't tell you. Being here is bending the rules. There is a thin line between keeping the balance and manipulating the outcome nature has decided. We cannot speak it aloud, but we can even the odds," Angele said gently.

"Will you trust us, for her sake?" Moll stepped forward.

Everything in him screamed trap. He should work on casting them out and strengthen his mental barrier. Except a lot of things he thought to be fact had been disproved. "All I ask for is a sign of good faith and intention."

"A witch's oath, sister?" Angele asked.

Moll inclined her head. "Yes, that will do."

The women moved to face one other, clasping hands. "We vow on our lives that no harm shall come to you from our hands. Every action taken will be for our common goal." A ripple of power filled the air. A golden hue surrounded them. He felt the spell settle in.

"Is that enough for you, vampire?" Moll asked with a sneer.

"That remains to be seen. Regardless, I'm willing to take the risk."

"Why?" Moll asked.

"For Nakeeta." He met her hostile gaze with an unflinching stare of his own. His prior ties had shifted. Nakeeta would come out of this alive. The mission had changed.

The women stepped forward and placed a hand on his shoulders. "Hold tight."

His teeth slammed together as his body convulsed. Pain exploded from every pore of his body. His knees buckled, and his vision went black.

"Crewe." He heard his name called from a long distance. The pain made him want to swim back toward the blackness. "Crewe." The distress in the sweet voice urged him to fight. Embracing the agony, he struggled toward the light at the end of a long tunnel. It felt like moving through hardening marshmallow. One step at a time, he watched the glowing circle grow larger. His bones and joints ached. Every nerve ending fired at once. It took everything in him not to give in and sleep.

He peered into the circle, that acted as a portal, showing him Keeta bent over his prone body. *How can I see this? What did those witches do to me?* She placed her hand, palm first, on his chest. A streak of power yanked him from the darkness and back into his body. His back arched and his body shook as his consciousness realigned with the present.

"Crewe?"

"Keeta?" he rasped. "What happened?"

"I don't know. You started to glow, and then you wouldn't wake up."

He pried his heavy lids open and focused on her distraught face. "You were worried about me then?"

"Yes. And now I'm starting to regret it."

He chuckled as he sat up. "A few of your witches paid me a visit." He tried to think back to their words.

"What did they want?"

"Funny, it's hard to remember now. I think it was to prove I was worthy of you." He ran his fingers through his hair. "How odd. We don't dream you know. I haven't experienced anything like this since before I was turned."

"What happens when you rest?"

He shrugged. "We turn off."

"That sounds rather terrifying."

"It's not as if I'm afraid I won't wake up," he stated, and rubbed his face. "You said I glowed?"

Sitting back on her knees, she nodded. "I woke up because I thought you'd turned on the lights, but you were levitating off the bed, emitting this bright white light. I had to squint my eyes to look at you. I tried to reach you, but there was a barrier." Her voice cracked. "I thought Genevie was retaliating."

"What changed your mind?" He raked his hands through his hair

"The inherent sense of goodness that came from the light. I just knew. It's hard to explain. It's a witch thing." She tugged at her earlobe.

"And yet not having dreams is strange? You are an odd breed." He propped the goose-feather pillows against the solid wood headboard, and leaned back.

"You never seemed to object to me." Balanced on her elbow, she searched his face.

"You, no. Everything with you has been different. The trust I've placed with you is personal, not linked to your kind." He ran his fingertips over her velvet skin, tracing her shoulder.

"You still distrust us?" Her plump lips turned down.

"Have your feelings changed on vampires?" He smoothed the red sheets down over his lap.

"No, but I'm willing to give them a chance to prove—"

"You shouldn't. It's dangerous and likely to get you killed."

She threw her hands in the air. "Then why are we even doing this?"

"Because we must. I did not say it was impossible, only that it will take time and proof. We aren't swayed so easily by words."

"I'm not a freakshow doing demonstrations for the crowd who pays for tickets." She wrapped her arms across her chest.

"You said you'd do what it took to convince others. It may come to that. We've been around long enough to see the start and end of many things. Rumors are ignored, and the things we see with our own eyes are picked apart."

"Because you want to be miserable?"

"Our nature is a suspicious one. It comes with the territory when your survival depends on staying hidden. You have evolved to live in the open. Us predators never could." He shook his head. "We'd be hunted to extinction. Humans fear what they don't understand, and if it's more powerful, they only learn enough to snuff out its life force or enslave it."

"Things have changed."

He chuckled darkly. "It's their very nature. Coded in their DNA. That's why we're in this mess in the first place. We didn't look like them, so we were monsters, spurned and hunted. We had to become predators to survive and find an acceptable existence."

"That was a choice your people made."

"As opposed to dwelling in dark, damp caves?" he challenged, rising to his feet. "Would you call that life?"

"You've earned your reputation."

"And witches are saints?"

"We try to *keep* the balance, not upset or take from it."

"Some. Not all," he said.

She ground her teeth together. "This isn't helping either of us." She exhaled.

"No," he agreed, curbing his temper. After centuries of defending them, he felt protective over his people.

"Are you sure you're okay?"

"You tell me."

Nodding, she held out her hand. Magic tickled his skin like the top of a feather as she scanned him from head to toe.

"I can't detect anything unusual. If you begin to feel strange, let me know immediately."

He gave a nod. "We need to get back to training. Every hour is precious."

"Stubborn mule," she mumbled.

"I'll take that as a compliment, witch."

She glanced over her shoulder. "You really shouldn't. I'll meet you at the maze. I'll warn you, I'm feeling rather lucky."

"I didn't figure you for the type to kick a man while he was down," he called to her retreating form as she left his room.

"What man?"

Her words made him roar with laughter. They were forming an understanding. It took time to overcome centuries of prejudice and distrust. Soon, they'd be placed under a microscope. Any sign of weakness would be exploited and used against them. There were a lot of holes that needed patches before they came under the scrutiny of his people. She was fire. Hot, passionate, savage, and responsive. His people were more like ice. Cool, level-headed, and manipulative. They played the long game. Letting loose on your tight reign of control, meant the beast inside took over, and then no one was safe. *A middle ground must be discovered fast, or we've lost before anyone has a chance to win.*

# Chapter Eight

They stood outside of the maze. Today she was pulling out the big guns. Rolling her neck, she relished the satisfying cracks. She could feel a danger coming in on the wind. Things were shifting, and their safe haven would become a thing of the past soon. Before that happened, she needed a win.

"Are you sure you're ready?" Crewe asked cockily.

She couldn't wait to watch that smug expression leave his face. *Arrogant bastard.* He had cause to be. He'd gotten used to being faster, stronger, and smarter. It would give anyone a superiority complex. He'd been teaching her his secrets as she learned to manage the changes happening to her body. Today she'd show him what a fast learner she truly was. For weeks, she'd suffered through a grueling training session, late night library searches, and constant corrections. It'd been a blow to her confidence.

Nothing she did felt right. Exhaustion became a way of life, and it was a struggle to keep the constant disappointment from becoming depression. They'd yet to discover the map or the notebook she'd seen in her vision. Every bit of information they'd gleaned about their situation felt like speculation or told them more of what they already knew. The situation was fast becoming dire.

Sorrow settled in her chest, a persistent ache like a bad cold one couldn't shake. Channeling her frustration, she pressed her lips into a thin line and nodded.

"Go." The words hardly left his mouth when she froze him in place.

His eyes widened, and she laughed as she took off, leaving an icy trail behind her on the ground. Gale force winds stirred her hair and clothing as they created a barrier between her and Crewe. Eyes on the prize, she leapt the hedges, pushing her body to the limits. The height of her jump stole her breath away. The blood had given her a strength that still frightened her.

Landing on the ground, she stumbled forward toward the white flag. She sensed Crewe closing the distance between them. *Not today.* Her fingers caught the stick. His scent flooded her. Snatching up the flag, she spun.

"And Bob's your uncle." Sweat dripped into her eyes and her lungs felt fit to burst, but she waved the white flag triumphantly.

"Proud of yourself, are you?" he asked with a smirk.

"Bested you, didn't I?"

"One captured flag does not a victory make."

"Oh-ho, who's a sore loser now?" she chuckled.

"Incorrigible."

"And you love it."

"Confident."

"Isn't that what you've groomed me to be? Like you?"

His mouth opened and closed as he faltered. "Is that how you feel?"

"Yes. How else could I walk in your world? You'll always be an enigma to me. Your brains are wired differently. I think the passage of time and the fact that you're all born when things were so different plays a part. I couldn't understand it if we weren't bonded." She shook her head.

"Do you see us differently, then?" The hopeful tone made her stomach tighten.

"I see *you* differently."

He opened his mouth and tensed.

"The wards have been breached." She sent her power out. "They yielded to the visitor." The scent tickled her nose—oakwood, moss, and masculine musk.

"Dregan is here."

A prickling made her hackles rise. "Magic?"

"He brought the witch," Crewe whispered. "Come."

"Like this?" She peered down at the sports bra and leggings.

"Yes, follow my lead." His nerves threw her off kilter. This wasn't the cool, calm, and collected man she'd grown used to. "*Remember everything I've taught you about our culture.*" His switch to their mental link raised the alarm. He didn't want Dregan to hear.

"*What's wrong?*" she asked.

"*Now is the time to prove ourselves. He'll be watching our every move. The fact that he brought his witch concerns me.*" He took off before she could ask anything more, and she followed suit. They approached the gates of the property and Crewe went down on one knee, bowing his head. She followed his lead and fell into a low sweeping curtsy, head to the ground. They were like wolves in that way. You didn't meet their gaze like you were an equal.

The raw power radiating from Dregan nearly made her dizzy. The man was ancient. She closed her eyes, adjusting to the waves flowing freely from him.

"Rise, Crewe."

"I apologize for our state. I did not realize you would arrive today."

"That is as it should be. I wanted to see *her* in her natural state. She moved like one of us."

"Yes."

Her stomach clenched, and she bit the inside of her cheek as they discussed her as if she weren't there. *Their ways are not your own.* She chanted the phrase in her head, keeping a tight grip on her emotions. Building an imaginary brick wall, she closed them in, clearing her face of the things she thought and felt. Channeling her best Resting Bitch Face, she focused on the conversation being held.

"Curious." Dregan inhaled. "Her scent is odd. Not quite witch or vampire. Does she drink blood?"

She tensed.

"She has on occasion."

*So, we're keeping our blood exchanges a secret.*

"And it doesn't make her ill?"

"I believe it helps her ... mimic us."

"Does she have fangs?"

"Not always."

"She doesn't like being spoken about instead of spoken to, Dregan," the sultry voice said.

"Ah, I forgot how ... *independent* witches can be. Rise, girl."

She flinched at the command. Digging her teeth into the flesh of her tongue, she stood ramrod straight, arms at her side, hands fisted.

"Oh, Morena, you were right. Look at her. I can smell the anger from here. Spicy and cinnamon. She's got a temper on her." His voice was a dark purr some would find attractive. It made her want to claw his eyes out. Dregan was tall, broad, and bearded. Careful not to meet his gaze head-on, she took him in. His golden blond hair tumbled around his shoulders, and his beard was braided and adorned with silver beads etched in runes. He cut an imposing figure as he towered above her. His eyes were a dark blue, unlike anything she'd ever seen.

His companion was beauty personified. Thick black hair waved its way down her back and around a round face with high cheekbones, an upturned nose, and full lips painted a cabernet color. Long, dark lashes framed down-turned black eyes. Her brown skin boasted Spanish descent along with her slight accent. Clad in a pair of black jeans, thigh high boots, and a black shirt, she looked runway ready.

"Blessed be, Nakeeta Alva." Morena bowed slightly.

"Blessed be," Keeta said softly, returning the gesture of respect.

"Polite. You've taught her well, Crewe."

"Thank you, sire."

"You can look at me, girl. I won't be using any of my powers on you." She met his cold gaze. "Our savior?" Doubt dripped from his tongue like acidic venom.

"So, they tell me."

His eyes widened. "Impertinent."

"Pardon me. Your ways are not my own. I am doing my best to be respectful, but I will not be cowed. I have left behind a life I worked hard to craft, changed the very core of my being, and I may well forfeit my life. I will not lose sight of who I am, too."

"Rebellious," he drawled.

"Honest and strong," Morena remarked softly.

"Not sorry," she said unapologetically.

*"What are you doing?"* Crewe's panicked voice reached her.

*"Being myself."*

"With all due respect, it's tradition, separation, and misunderstandings that have landed us in this mess. Doing things the way we've always done them won't fix the problem. I've been chosen to change everything, and that's what I plan on doing." 'Whether you like it or not' was inferred, though she never said the words aloud.

Dregan's nostrils flared, and his eyes took on a menacing expression that reminded her of the berserkers of lore. His eyebrows came together, and his thin lips curled up into a sneer.

"Suddenly you're the messiah for the races?"

"I didn't ask for this. I was given the task, and I'll be damned if I fail.

There's no pride involved. Only the desire for survival." She kept her tone as even as possible as she delivered the information factually.

"She's right," Morena said softly. "This is about more than which race is more powerful or refined. She's caught in the middle of things she didn't cause. Anger is not to be taken out on her." Her words appeared to penetrate his anger. *Who is this woman?*

His lids lowered, shutting down the simmering rage. "You're right, of course. Old habits, they die hard. We must come together because the alternative is unthinkable."

Dregan didn't apologize, but she hadn't expected him to. Instead, they formed a tentative truce.

"Show me what you've learned."

She glanced down at Crewe. "Now?"

"Is there a better time?" He pulled the Medieval broadsword from his scabbard.

"Sire—" Crewe began.

"You won't always be there to run interference," Dregan said, silencing him before he could speak further.

Morena handed her a sword, and she tested the weight, familiarizing herself with a few strikes as she took the proper stance.

"You look the part," Dregan observed. "Now let's see if you have any skills." He moved like a snake, striking out with precision and speed. Her sword scarcely blocked his. She thrust forward, only to catch air as he danced away. His movements were too fast for the human eye to track, but she could see the blur. She stepped back on her left foot, turning her body to avoid his attack. Her blood boiled. Dregan meant to land a blow. He had age and skill on his side. *I'd best even the odds.* She upturned the earth. Dregan stumbled, and she swung her sword. He barely avoided her thrust as he leapt away.

A whirling attack of blades, heavy blows, and skillful thrusts forced her on a defensive run. She'd poked the bear, and he was responding in anger.

He brought his sword down. She blocked. The momentum behind the blow brought her to her knees. Her arms shook. *Solis.* A brilliant flash of sunlight made him cry out. Dropping his sword, he covered his eyes. She scrambled away. It was enough to shock him, without injuring. He turned his red eyes to her, and the sight of his elongated fangs woke true fear.

The predator came to life before her eyes. His fangs dripped with saliva, and his height seemed to grow. Her heart thudded in her chest. Tossing the sword to the ground, she lifted her hands. Magic crackled between her fingers. The bluish-green glow comforted her. She had the means to defend herself. The beast inside of her roared, and she hissed.

"By Odin's Beard. Her eyes," Dregan mumbled. The wards screamed a warning as they were rent open, and a flaming ball of red energy hit the ground inches from where she stood. The explosion threw up dirt and grass. Knocked off her feet, she tucked and landed in a roll as muscle memory took over. Coming to a stop, she dug her fingers in the ground.

"We've been followed!" Morena cried. A blast of dark energy swept her off her feet. Smoke flooded the space, obscuring the ground, making it harder to distinguish friend from foe. She could smell a mix of vampires, witches, and … Her nose twitched. Wolves!

"*What's happening?*" She sent the panicked words through their link.

"*An ambush.*"

"*Who?*"

"*I don't know.*" His hand grabbed hers. "*We leave now, alone. I won't trust the wrong person.*" She cried out as a dark shape dive bombed him. His fist smashed into the wolf's face, sending it flying.

"*At my back.*" She pressed her back to his, hands up and ready. *Somnum.* A bolt of energy and a sharp command stopped an overeager wolf in his tracks. He slumped to the ground, unconscious. Air circulation cut off as an invisible hand grasped her around the throat and squeezed. Her fingers dug into thin air instinctively as she battled the spell. Breaking the hold, she sucked in air.

Slammed into from the side, she hit the ground hard enough to see stars. Spells were flung from every angle, giving her no time for recovery.

She struggled to raise a shield spell as the wolves converged. A brilliant red flame surrounded her, setting the ground around her ablaze that erupted into a wall of flame. Shielded, she sought the source of the magic.

"Stay away from my mate."

"Crewe!" A sonic boom made her clutch her ears. The flames died down, and her jaw dropped. Enemies littered the ground.

"We leave now." Crewe drew her into her arms and leapt into the air. A scream spilled free from her lips as they took to the sky. Wrapping her legs and arms around him tightly, she buried her face in his neck.

*"You can fly?"*

*"Apparently, I as you kids say, leveled up."*

*"This is the first time you've done this?"* Even through their mental link, her voice sounded shrill.

*"Would you rather be back there in battle?"*

*"No."* She'd never hated his ability to sound calm and collected more. *"Where are we going?"*

*"As far as I can manage to take us and then we'll stop and rest, and you'll perform a spell to prevent me from being tracked. Now, be quiet so I can concentrate."*

She mentally slammed her mouth shut. The last thing she needed to do was end up in the middle of the ocean in the dark.

## CREWE

He brought them down in a hilly countryside devoid of buildings. She'd fallen asleep against him mid-flight. He'd seen powerful masters able to take to the skies, but he'd never imagined he would possess the skill. They had yet to speak of it, but he'd worked magic. When he'd seen her about to get attacked, a flip had switched on inside of him. Power, unlike anything he'd experienced before surged up and out. *It seems I'm not the only one who's been changed by our exchanges.* Trailing his fingers across her cheek, he bent down and kissed her forehead. One more moment of peace, before reality.

Settling her in her his lap, he nuzzled her neck, inhaling her scent, and reminding himself why he'd left his sire to fight alone on the battlefield. He didn't want to believe Dregan would betray them, but Kazimir had warned him not to trust anyone. So far he'd been proven honest.

"Mmmhmm."

"Time to wake up. We have spells to cast, and people to outrun."

Her eyelids fluttered open. She jerked, looking around.

"We're on the ground."

"Oh, thank you, Jesus."

"Was the flight that bad?"

"No, but as it was your first, I felt like a crash test dummy."

"I would never let you fall." He brushed his lips with hers. "Dregan can track me through our bond."

"And I need to block that." She sat up straight, wiggling in his lap until her legs lay on either side of his thighs. Cupping his face, she rested her forehead against his and hummed as she slipped into his mind and traveled along their bond. *"Show me."* He led her to the link that bound him to his adopted sire. The dark red cord pulsed with life. She placed her hand on it and began to sing as she drew a triangle over the link, infusing it with her power. She drew a block inside of the triangle and turned the colorful neon green symbol left three times. Lifting her hand, she slammed her palm flat onto the block.

Shuddering, he felt the instant sense of being alone. The bond had connected him to the others of his line.

"Are you okay?" She leaned back.

"Yes. It's … disorienting. I'll be fine." He could feel the pull of the sun. "We must seek shelter. The sun will rise in three hours."

"What do we do?"

"First, we need to figure out where we are. I may have friends willing to help."

"Won't they tell Dregan?" she whispered.

"Not everyone answers to a sire. Many vampires prefer to act as lone wolves. Connected to the community, but beholden to no one."

"Isn't that lonely?"

He rose, placing her on her feet. "No. They have friends, but their allegiances are to themselves." He took her hand. "Come." Entwining their fingers, he led her toward the sleeping minds he sensed in the distance. Slipping in past their nonexistent mental defenses he found a location. "We're in the city of Rye in East Sussex."

"What should we do?"

"I know someone. I apologize for what comes next, but it's a necessary evil. Where we're going, knowing what you are would be dangerous."

"Where are you taking me?"

"To the underground. You'll need to pose as my blood slave."

She pulled away. "No."

He grabbed her wrist and squeezed. "They would sell you to the highest bidder, and I shudder to think what that person would do to you. Do you understand what I'm saying?"

"What do I need to do?"

"Don't ask questions, pretend to be in a daze, and keep your ears peeled for danger. Save the communication for our bond."

"And if someone approaches me?"

He growled at the thought. "I'll handle that."

"Okay." She sounded shell-shocked.

"I know a lot has happened, but I will get us through this."

She nodded.

"Come. We have no time to waste." He scooped her into his arms and took off toward the market. Under the slumbering city, a world was alive with action.

Trading of spells, hexes, and blood exchange were among a few of the hot commodities available. They were outcasts. People who lived as they chose in lieu of the way society suggested they behave. Much like the human society, they had their quirks and versions of right and wrong. He clutched Keeta to his side as they traversed the dark pathways.

They entered the bustling market. Stalls filled the rows. Witches with dried herbs displayed their wares beside vampires with blood on ice in IV bags. In the center on stage, men and women were auctioned off. Vampires waved their number as a lithe blonde turned slowly. Her fear was intoxicating. She trembled as the crowd salivated, and a bidding war began.

"*What the hell is that?*"

"*Exactly what you think it is.*" Crewe scanned the area in search of a familiar head of strawberry blond curls. He spotted his target. Slipping through the throng of people, he touched the vampire's shoulder.

"Sandor."

"Surely my ears deceive me. This cannot be Crewe I hear." The man spun and smiled. His hazel eyes filled with mirth. He twirled the thin end of his mustache. "And yet look at you. With a *special* guest no less."

"Everyone needs a break now and then, Sandor."

"You're a few millennia overdue if you ask me," Sandor said silkily. He straightened the lapels of his gray suit. "What brings you here?"

"We need safe passage to America."

Sandor nodded toward Keeta. "Steal her, did you?"

"It's not my fault some people don't recognize the goldmines they're sitting on." Crewe shrugged his shoulders, careful to keep his emotions hidden.

Sandor smirked. "She's not your everyday blood slave I take it?" His eyes darkened, and he licked his lips.

Crewe bared a bit of fang. "No. She's mine. We both know I don't share. So, you can understand why I'd like to get her," he glanced around, "situated away from prying eyes."

Throwing his head back, Sandor laughed. "When you break the rules, you certainly go all out. I do believe I owe you a favor. Come, let us make arrangements." He strode away and gestured for them to follow. Crewe casually observed the crowd, careful not to draw attention to himself, while keeping his guard up. It'd be the last place he was expected, but news could travel fast. The farther away from the crowd they got, the more he relaxed. They wound their way through a labyrinth of stone passageways until they reached a wooden door. He tapped a series of rhythmic knocks, and it opened.

"If you want to travel incognito, the first thing you must do is get out of those rags. I don't judge, but I do speak the truth." Sandor swept his arm toward the entryway, bidding them enter. Crew stepped through first, stunned by the fully furnished living room complete with a comfortable couch, fifty-inch flat screen television, expensive artwork, and wooden tables.

"One needs a plethora of hidey holes when the sun is unkind," Sandor explained with a shrug.

"Venett." He nodded his head at Sandor's partner in crime. The dark-haired vampire with Betty Paige bangs, and a slinky black dress resembled a Gothic teen. It was the perfect guise for the centuries-old vampire.

"Crewe."

"Can you assist his … guest, Venett?" Sandor asked.

Her nose twitched, and her eyes turned red.

"Fangs to yourself, dear one. I know she's mouthwatering, but she's not for us."

Venett pouted. "Pity. We'll get you cleaned up, dressed to impress, and on a private jet in no time, darling."

"And should anyone ask after me?" Crewe said before she could walk away.

"Who'd believe you were in the underground for anything other than work, Crewe? Your secret shall remain safe with us," Venett replied.

"My word is never questioned here. You know that." Sandor waved his hand dismissively. Here he was king.

Keeta glanced at him. *"Should I go with her?"*

*"Go. You'll be safe."*

She followed the female vampire back into their rooms.

Crewe nodded. "My thanks, old friend." He clapped his hand.

Sandor grinned. "I rather like this rebellious streak you've discovered. I want to see how it will play out." He sat down in a leather lazy boy and crossed his leg over his knee.

"Still as wicked as ever," Crew mused.

"You say the nicest things." Sandor beamed. "Your pretty little blood donor oozes power."

"She does," he agreed, giving away nothing more.

"Keeping your cards close to your sleeve, are you? Curious." Sandor tapped a finger to his cheek.

Crewe shrugged. "Says the man with a million secrets."

"You never fail to play the game well. It's a pity you won't join us down here. You could have a good, lucrative life."

"I won't leave one master for another. You're lenient, but I'd be working for you, nonetheless."

"Do you fancy yourself an entrepreneur then?"

"I'm not sure what I am yet, Sandor," Crewe sighed.

"That means you're ready for reinvention. And I have to say it's about time."

Venett cleared her throat. "If I can have your attention, gentleman. May I introduce the new and improved Ms.K."

The black leather pants looked painted onto her shapely legs and lovingly hugged her plump ass. Knee-high black boots gave her additional height and went with the chic black, off-the-shoulder sweater that showed an expanse of her slender neck and collarbone. She'd tamed her hair, weaving it into an intricate French braid, and tossed it over her opposite shoulder. Crewe stood and stepped forward, entranced.

"I think he likes your work, darling," Sandor said. His voice sounded distant.

*"If you're trying to feign nonchalance, you're failing."* The amusement in her mental voice snapped him back to the present.

"You've done well, Venett."

"Now let's give you the same treatment. We don't want people thinking you've kidnapped the poor woman." Sandor swept past them, and he reluctantly followed the red-haired man down a small hallway.

"I've been dying to get my hands on you in one way another."

*That's what I'm afraid of.*

✤ ✤

"I THINK YOU GOT THE raw end of the deal here."

"It was killing you not to say anything, wasn't it?" He tugged at the leather pants.

"Oh, yeah." She turned to face him in the plush white leather seats of the private jet. "You vamps sure travel in style."

"We've had enough time to accumulate wealth. It'd be silly not to use it to our advantage." He loosened the black scarf with skulls around his neck and tried to ignore the tight fit of the borrowed clothing.

"Spoken like a wealthy person." Keeta ran her fingers down his scarf. "Do you think he'll rat us out?"

"No, he's very anti-establishment." Bending down, he placed a kiss on her crown. "I think we'll be safe for our flight. Once we reach Savannah, we'll have an entirely new set of worries."

"Why trust Kaz? Look what happened already."

He wrapped an arm around her shoulders and pulled her to him. "He told me to be careful who I trusted. I don't know if Dregan was involved in this. I don't want him to be, but the sickness does things to our mind." He shook his head. "Either way, we have nowhere else to go. We need to regroup, plan, and moved forward."

"I have friends—"

"They'll be expecting us to go back to Louisiana."

"There are more ways than one to contact family."

"Enough, witch. Turn off your big brain and rest." He pulled her head down to his shoulder.

"I can't."

Burying his fingers in her hair, he captured her lips, silencing her with a blistering kiss. He broke the kiss to let her breathe. "We're alive, and no one knows where we are. For now, it's enough."

"Bossy vampire." The words were muffled, but he understood them well enough.

"Stubborn witch."

# Chapter Nine

### KEETA

SHE FOLLOWED HIS DIRECTIONS, PLACING thick comforters over the blackout curtains they'd taken from the plane. *Vamps really do think of everything.* With no real plan, they'd checked into the Hotel Indigo in the historic district. The old, brick building and the area appealed to Crewe, who'd pulled money from a private account he'd kept hidden from everyone. With the room sufficiently Crewe ready, she sat on the end of the bed. The city was old. The ancestral magic hummed beneath their feet. Intricate spells woven over time blazed to life the moment they landed. It was a warning system.

She felt like she was constantly walking through cobwebs. The feeling of thin strands of energy brushing up against her barriers made her shudder.

"This place is alive with magic," Crewe marveled.

"You feel it, too?" Her mouth parted as she studied his pensive face, stunned at his keen observation. Too much sat between them unsaid.

"Yes. It's the oddest sensation." He frowned. "How can you stand it?"

"Most places aren't so active. I suppose you get used to it. It's part of being connected to everything. When the balance is thrown off, you feel it here," she placed a hand on her belly, "and here," and another over her heart.

"No wonder you strive to keep the balance. It affects you on a personal level." He tilted his head to the side as the wheels in his head spun at a furious pace. She could almost see the mechanisms whirling.

"Yes." She took one of his hands between hers and ducked her head to meet his gaze. "Now you begin to fully understand. What we do isn't a judgment call. We work to keep things at an even keel because it is in our nature, and serves our best interest."

"What different creatures we are." He shook his head. Sadness tinged his aura a deep blue. "You act to preserve for everyone, and we act to protect ourselves."

"As you've said, we've been able to walk in the open for a lot longer. I think on some level we're all formed by the things our ancestors went through. It's coded deep into our bones, influencing us even as we evolve. Perhaps escaping who we once were is a futile endeavor."

He grunted. "I hope you're wrong. Because otherwise, we're all doomed."

"I don't believe that."

Slipping his hand from hers, he trailed his thumb across her cheekbones. "Then you'll have to believe for both of us, witch. Because I find myself running low on optimism. Are we going to approach the elephant in the room?"

She snickered. "Always to the point."

"What happened at the castle?" He cupped the back of his neck. "That power I wielded wasn't normal."

"When has anything between us been considered the norm?" she teased.

"I used a witch's magic. Have you ever heard of that happening before?"

"No. I don't think they'd be advertising it, though."

"You're right, of course." He chuckled self-deprecatingly. "It makes one incredibly dangerous. A weapon to be used or a threat to be extinguished."

"What happened?" she whispered.

"I saw you on the ground about to be attacked by wolves, and I knew I couldn't get to you in time. Anger unlike anything I've ever experienced swept through me and something inside of me snapped." He furrowed his brow. "Or perhaps is clicked into place."

"May I examine you?"

He swallowed hard and nodded.

She stood. Palms up, she scanned him—starting at the top of his head, she gently prodded his aura. It was altered.

"Wow." What was once black had become a deep blue. Shimmery bits that looked like stars were scattered haphazardly. The points pulsed with power.

"What do you see?"

"You're beautiful. Like a night sky. Your aura has changed. It's as if you were part witch."

"Maybe I am. In the same way you are no longer simply a witch." He gripped her hips, pulling her between his legs.

Hands on his shoulders, she leaned back. "Now it's you who must learn control."

"And you love that, don't you?"

"Perhaps a little." She bent and nipped at his bottom lip. "I think we need to take our mind off things."

"What did you have in mind?" He widened his eyes, feigning innocence.

She laughed darkly. "Why don't you guess?" Wrapping her arms around his neck, she swung her left leg over his, and he pressed his other leg together, lifting her to sit on his lap.

"A hug?" He hooked his arms around her, pulling her closer.

"That's a start." She nodded her head, pleased he decided to play along. Since meeting, they'd been in a constant state of upheaval, high-stress situations, and peril. They needed this. Every smile felt like a gift. For so long, he'd had only death and missions. She wanted to show him there was more.

He licked her pulse point. Her body tensed and she rolled her hips against the bulge in his pants. His fingers dug into her hips as he nipped his way down her neck. Each bite was harder than the next, but he never broke the skin. Whimpering, she pressed her neck more firmly into his mouth. His chuckle vibrated through her. Her breath caught, and her belly clenched.

Twining his fingers in her curls, he tugged sharply. The pull on her scalp pushed her closer to the edge.

"You're so pretty when you submit." His words sent a hot river flowing between her legs. "Oh, you like that, do you?" His accent thickened as he nipped her bottom earlobe. "You like it when I claim what's mine?" Fangs caressed the tender flesh of her neck. She panted, trembling as she waited for his next move. "Because you are. You understand that, don't you?"

Dazed, she tilted her head up to meet his ruby gaze. "I'm what?" she whispered.

"Mine." The possession in his eyes caressed her like a lover.

"I don't recall being asked." That she managed to form the words was a small miracle.

"Stubborn witch. Shall I show you what your body already knows?" He rocked her against him. "See how your body sings? How your honey flows?" He inhaled. "You smell like a ripe grapefruit sprinkled with sugar … red and juicy." His fingers slipped under her shirt, and caressed the skin on her back, setting her aflame. "Arms up, my mouthy little love."

He mesmerized her. Clothing hit the ground with a gentle whoosh as she obeyed his sensual commands.

"Hmmm, suddenly you're quiet, love."

He bit into her neck, and she saw stars. Bright points of light exploded behind her lids. Her back arched. One sip had her tumbling over the edge into bliss. Tremors continued to make her muscles twitch. She opened her eyes and found herself spread out before him like a buffet.

"So, this is how to hush your backtalk?"

"You—" He drove home, and she cried out, all responses forgotten.

Digging her nails into his shoulders, she wrapped her legs around him, pressing her heels into his back as she matched him stroke for stroke. The friction melted her brain as they moved in a sensual rhythm that took her higher and higher. He filled her to bursting and retreated. Their bond broke open. She fell into a loop of pleasure as his emotions became her own.

Her mouth watered as her smaller fangs distended.

*"That's it, witch. Bite me."* He moved her hips, going deeper as she sank her fangs into his neck and they both shattered. Her body convulsed, clenching him tight as he continued to drive his way through her own completion. Swallowing his sweet blood, she trembled as desire rocketed through her.

She screamed, breaking the suction as she experienced his completion and felt his essence coat her insides. Spent, they collapsed side by side on the bed as she struggled to catch her breath. He rolled to face her. Turning her head, she smiled.

"I love thee, Nakeeta." His words were softly spoken and completely heartfelt, expressed in the language of his time.

"And I love you, Crewe." She brought her heavy arm up to caress his baby fine hair. Memorizing the moment, she held it close to her heart. There was pure joy to be had here among the wreckage of their old lives. It gave them more reason to succeed.

❈ ❈

"I THINK THEY'VE FOUND US," Keeta whispered groggily. The low-level wards she placed around their building woke her from a light slumber. Pushing herself up onto her elbow, she rubbed her face.

"Kaz said they would."

"Let's hope the rest of what he promised was true," she mumbled.

He squeezed her shoulder. "Let us make ourselves presentable for our guests."

She watched the walls come back up as he took on his vampire persona.

Knowing what lay behind his mask, she'd never be able to see him as others did. As she trailed her fingers down his strong jawline, she drew strength from their bond as she slowly moved from the bed to straighten her hair, wash her face, and steady her nerves. In borrowed clothes, she felt like a child playing dress up. Black skinny jeans and a black T-shirt with the lunar cycle around the word 'Moonchild' wasn't an outfit that commanded respect. *It did allow a person to blend in, though.*

Turning on the tap, she let the sound of running water soothe her senses as she brushed her teeth. She splashed the cold water on her face. The shock of the temperature made her flinch. Spinning the faucet, she froze. Misty whiteness coated the mirror. A hazy cloud gathered as she breathed. The intense sensation of being watched set in.

Attention drawn to the mirror, she focused on the large square with a swirling silver design patinaed by age. A line appeared in the condensation. She jumped back. More followed, spelling out the word 'look'. The mirror rippled outward, like a pond disturbed by a pebble. Slowly, a hand emerged from the mirror. Long, slender, brown fingers clutched a faded and worn brown notebook.

Trembling, she reached for the article, powers ready to block. Mirrors were portals in the hands of the powerful. The last thing she needed to do was land in another dimension. The hand remained benign, as she took the lightweight book from it. Returning from where it came, the temperature of the room rose, and the crawling sensation on her skin ceased. The door slammed open. Crewe rushed in with a motley couple behind him.

"Are you okay?" Crewe cupped her face.

She gripped his forearms. "I'm fine."

"We felt an ancient source coming from this room. It barred us from entering." She glanced over at the petite redhead with a short bob, dark brown eyes, and porcelain skin. Her round eyes and delicate facial structure gave her a doll-like appearance. But she sensed her age.

"How long was I in here?" she asked, taking the time to observe the tall, olive-skinned man with thick, chestnut-colored hair that framed his square face, and highlighted his wide-set moss green eyes. He seemed laid-back, but his magic was strong.

"Fifteen minutes too long," Crewe snapped.

"Wow. For me, it was seconds."

"I'm starting to think I can't leave you alone."

She scowled. "For once, we got a break." Grinning, she waved the book she'd seen in her vision. *"I see you decided to trust Kaz."*

*"I can't explain how, but I knew."* His baffled voice in her mind made her giggle.

*"Welcome to the witchy world, Crewe."*

"Keeta. This is Lavina and Reagan. They are here as ambassadors for The Balance."

"They match us, a witch and a vampire."

Reagan laughed. The rich sound coaxed an answering smile from her. "Oh, she's going to be a breath of fresh air." His southern drawl was as sweet as sugar when it broke over her ears.

"We have serious things to discuss," Lavina replied sternly.

"Doesn't mean we have to be as dull as a pile of rocks while we do it, Lav." Regan stepped forward. "It's a pleasure to make your acquaintance. We've been waiting a long time for this."

"Is he for real?" Keeta whispered.

"She doesn't understand who she is," Lavina said in a voice tinged with sadness.

"Crewe?" She turned to him, and he shook his head.

"You are the Mother. The blood of the three beings runs through your veins. Everything started with your line, and it will end or continue with it."

The impact of the words made her knees shake. Images of the Native American played in her heart. The murders, cannibalism, and careful consumption of the hearts. He'd twisted the gifts given, and now they would all pay. *Unless I do something.*

"I don't know what to do."

"That's where we come in. And that book. We've heard rumors of the Seer journal, but we weren't sure it truly existed," Reagan whispered.

"Seer journal?"

"There was a woman who foretold what would come, and her visions were recorded and kept safe. Or so the story went." Lav's eyes were glued to the yellowed-paper journal in Keeta's hand.

Directing her gaze down at the book, she opened it and watched as the ink appeared on the paper.

*My name is Blythe Rivet, and for a long time, I thought I was crazy. Until I understood why I truly am, and what my role is to play. If you're reading this, things are worse than I ever anticipated they'd be.*

"It's true." Keeta's voice shook.

"Let me see." Lav grabbed the book. "Shit." She jumped back, waving her red hands. "It was like sticking my hands in a fire."

"Because it wasn't meant for you," she read the words appearing in the book. "Only the chosen can access the books. It's a fail-safe."

"Chosen?"

"There's more than one of me … er, us. One from each bloodline. The map will lead us to them."

"Where's the map?" Crewe asked.

"I haven't gotten that far yet."

"We can't stay here in the open like this. It's not safe. Eyes and ears are always about, reporting back to their masters," Reagan stated.

Crewe placed himself slightly in front of her. "Where do you suggest we go?"

"Someplace safe, warded, well-hidden, and protected by the rest of us."

"How many of there are you?" Keeta inquired.

"Six. Three witches and three vampires," Lav replied.

"If you're deceiving us, you'll regret it." The ruthless tone sent shivers of delight down Keeta's spine. In a world gone mad, knowing her vampire was formidable did funny things to her insides.

"Her eyes," Reagan muttered.

Reining the emotion in, Keeta averted her gaze.

"Beautiful, aren't they?" Crewe asked.

"You are very protective of your ward," Lav remarked, cocking his head to the side.

"She is my mate."

Lav's dark brown eyes widened. "Is that such a wise choice given her importance?"

A snarling growl rumbled in his chest. "If you try to come between us, you will not like the end result."

"Distractions are dangerous and lead to mistakes," Lav stated.

"I wasn't aware that sharing a safe haven made you our leader. If this is the case, I respectfully decline. You see, I was alive and, on the battlefield, before you were a thought. Among your circle, you may be old, young one, but I am your elder a dozen times over." He stood taller as the icy haughtiness decimated her. Lavina shrank back under his glower.

"She gets the picture, vampire. Now is not the time to play who has the biggest dick. You'd win by default." Reagan's dry humor broke the staring contest.

Lavina bristled as she lowered her gaze. Crewe's shoulders relaxed slightly.

"I came to you because of Kaz. My faith is in him, not you. Don't pretend to know me, what I'm capable of, or how dedicated I am to the cause. Keeta is mine. Accept it and treat her according to our customs, or we will come to blows sooner rather than later."

A thrill swept through her as he staked his claim. The pride and possessiveness burned brightly through their bond. She took a fighting stance behind him, lending her silent support, and showing despite her vampire's high-handed ways, she was no weakling.

Clenching her teeth, Lavina gave a stiff vow. "We have an understanding."

Crewe nodded. "Then we shall proceed."

### CREWE

HE DIDN'T LIKE THE ODDS. They were two people, facing six. He had no clue how powerful the other witches or vampires were. Lavina was two hundred years old, and what she lacked in years, she made up for with the chip on her shoulder. He carefully noted the directions as they left the city behind and wound their way through the city in the Navy-blue SUV with blacked-out windows. Keeta remained beside him, silent as she slowly flipped her way through the aging papers of the journal. The scent of aged parchment, old ink, saline, and desperation unnerved him. The item felt cursed. Slowly, he moved his hand closer, waiting for the burn. His fingers touched the leather.

*"You and I are one. Of course, it wouldn't hurt you."* Keeta's admonishment made him smirk mentally. She'd come so far from their first encounter in the hospital room. He admired the woman she'd become. Returning his attention to the drive, he tensed. Pressure on his skin made him shift in his seat.

"You feel it so strongly?" Reagan asked

"Feel what?" He memorized the feeling, gathering information like intel for a battle.

"The wards." Lavina peered at him through the back mirror.

"Yes."

"Curious," Reagan muttered.

"Why?"

"Because you're responding as a witch would," Keeta said quietly.

"Are you finding anything interesting in there?" Lavina asked.

"That's one way of putting it."

The weariness in her reply put him on alert.

*"What?"*

"*This will require tedious rituals. I'll need to go through a purification process, a full moon.*" She paused. Apprehension flooded him.

"*What?*" he asked impatiently.

"*You won't like it. I'll need to perform blood magic.*"

He flinched. "*Isn't that dark?*"

"*It's a gray area that's hinged on intentions.*"

"*You're downplaying how dangerous it can be.*" Anger rose. "*Do not hold things back from me.*"

"*Okay.*"

Unconvinced by her tone, he grabbed her chin and forced her to meet his gaze. "*I meant it.*"

"*So, you are the only one allowed to protect me? Never the other way around?*" The ire in her voice amused him.

"*When the fate of the world rests on you, yes. We can fight over dominance after this is over.*"

Huffing, she jerked from his grasp and lifted the book to block his view. Sending her laughter through their link, he kept his attention on their *guides* and the surroundings. They'd long left the city and twisted their way through the countryside. The intensity of the wards told him they were nearing their final destination. Moving deeper into a forested area, the trees grew together overhead, giving them additional shelter from the sun's rays.

"Do you move around during the day?" He wanted to take stock of what these people were capable of.

"Yes, more and more often now." The concern in Lavina's voice matched his own.

The sun's rays chased them farther into the depths of the forest. They turned off the main road onto a private drive. The press of others became noticeable. He could feel them, waiting at their final destination. There was no animosity he could sense. This new skill would take getting used to. In a world bent on hiding emotions, being able to sense the will of others felt like a gross invasion of privacy.

"We chose this property because the land was unkempt and overgrown. Most have forgotten the house existed." After a ten-minute drive through an urban jungle, the two-story, plantation style home with a wraparound porch came into view. Painted a garish pink, it reminded him of a Barbie home.

"The girls won the color vote," Reagan muttered, glumly.

"And yet, you never let us forget it, so did we really win?" Lavina countered.

"It looks like a Barbie house!" Keeta sat up straight and pressed her nose to the window. Her delight was contagious. His lips twitched upward.

"It's the perfect cover for a group of witches and vampires, no? At best, they think we're eccentric artists. Everyone forgives your oddities once they realize you're artistic." Lavina's voice swelled with pride.

"We occasionally sell paintings and sculptures in town. It keeps our story realistic, and they never know we've woven spells into them," Regan added.

"What kind?" Crewe asked.

"Protective and monitoring. They give us a heads up on who comes into our town, and ward off most others." Regan supplied the answers as they drove into an empty space among other cars and turned the engine off.

"Who creates the art?" Keeta asked.

"Cian and Silver do the painting. Lavina and I work with clay. Sculptures and pottery mostly. Rainer knits, and Cyprian creates the most incredible jewelry as well as paints."

"You've created a cozy haven for yourself," Crewe said.

"We've done all right," Reagan replied evenly.

"The others are waiting anxiously." Lavina turned into her seat. "Are you prepared to meet them?"

"The sooner we get the ball rolling, the better." Keeta closed her book and sat up straight. "Surely, you feel the urgency I do."

"I think you are directly connected to the events and it affects you differently." Reagan's word was thoughtful.

"Regan has a special talent for seeing things that aren't obvious to the rest of us," Lavina explained.

Crewe opened the door and helped her down. Eyes scanning the property, he followed Lavina and Reagan, keeping his body between them and Keeta. Though it pricked her pride, she allowed him to take the lead. The door opened into a large entryway where the others stood lined up to greet them. They ranged in height, shape, ethnicity, and hair colors. Each had their own personalities. From the long, silvery purple locks of the willowy vampire, to the white blond-haired witch with a mohawk dressed in ripped jeans and an old Nirvana shirt, they appeared to be at ease with themselves and each other. An impressive feat.

The petite brunette with the short pixie-cut stepped forward. Her pale pink cupid's bow lips were curved into a smile, and her almond-shaped, amber-colored eyes welcomed them warmly.

"I'm Rainer. It's lovely to meet you and your mate."

He quirked an eyebrow.

"I see auras, and yours blend together," Rainer answered the unspoken question. "The blond behemoth is Cian. He's terrifying but kind, I assure you." The arctic blue eyes studying them made Crewe doubt her statement.

Cian bowed slightly. "It's a pleasure to meet you." His voice held a faint Eastern European accent. There was a sense that didn't fit with the image he portrayed. The discrepancy made him uneasy. He placed his hand on Keeta's hip behind him, refusing to let her come closer.

"I have extended my life many times," he explained.

"Wow." Keeta's head popped out from behind him. "That's rare."

Cian smiled. "It's a family secret." There was more to his story than he let on.

"Our resident purple-haired princess is Silver," Rainer continued.

"I am starting to understand how the house came to be pink," Crewe said.

Silver let out a tinkling laugh. "Oh, he might be a bit of all right."

Her British accent told him she hailed from Yorkshire.

"Quite the eclectic group you've gathered." Crewe wasn't sure how to feel about that. It wasn't in vampires to reach out of their comfort zone and befriend others.

"When people have a similar, peculiar interest, they tend to end up in the same circle," the man at the end spoke with a cool, French-accented voice.

"Last but not least this is Cyprian." The vampire was no more than five-foot-seven inches, but the aura of power he possessed made him seem twice that size. Long, black hair was pulled back into a ponytail, leaving his delicate features on display. His thin lips curled up in a smile.

"It's an honor to meet you, Crewe. Though I wish it weren't under such circumstances."

"You know me, vampire?"

"Your reputation and that of your sire precede you. I make a point of knowing major players."

"It's a smart thing to do." Vampires respected power.

"Oui."

"You are the thing that pulls us all together, Mother," Rainer said. Crewe watched on, stunned as they knelt before her.

"You wondered what bound us. Hope that this moment would come. We've prepared for this for years. Rainer is a seer. She found us and assembled our family. We will swear a blood oath to our fealty if you wish it."

He turned to see Lavina smile sadly. "Our mission is too important to let quibbles get in the way of success."

"Rise. I am no better than any of you." Keeta's voice rang out. "It was separation and superiority that got us here. I am honored that each of you are willing to help. We've much work to do."

"She has the seer's journal," Silver's voice said in awe.

"The next moon we must perform the revealing ritual to find the map. It will lead us to the others who will help me repair and recast the spell."

"You've seen it?" Cian asked.

"No. All four of us must be together for that."

"Brilliant," Silver whispered.

"Indeed," Crewe agreed.

"The next full moon is in a week," Cyprian added.

"Good. We'll need that entire time to prepare. It requires purification and a lot of magic. We'll need to be well rested and well fed."

"It's finally happening," Rainer whispered. She closed her eyes and placed a hand on her heart. "There were times I thought perhaps I'd been wrong about what I saw."

Keeta stepped from behind him and placed a gentle hand on Rainer's shoulder. "You aren't crazy. Without you, none of this would have come to pass."

Rainer grasped Keeta's forearms and a moment passed between the two.

"Well, let's not be rude to our guests, we'll show them their rooms."

Crewe scowled at Lavina.

"Room," she amended.

He nodded, and the others laughed.

The urge to have her to himself was strong. He bit his tongue as she took the time to shake the hand of each person, and speak with them personally. They looked at her as if she hung the moon. He supposed in a way she did. It amazed him how easily she fell into her role. She smiled gently, nodding as she responded, giving them her total attention. Benevolence and humility weren't things he'd seen much of.

*Perhaps we had it all wrong.*

"She's not going anywhere. How about we let them settle in?" Lavina said.

"About that. I don't have much of my own," Keeta stated, sheepishly. "We left in a bit of a rush."

"*Understatement.*"

"*Shut up. Do you want to remain in leather pants?*"

He decided not to respond.

"*Thought so.*" Her smug retort amused him. She'd picked up more than a desire for blood from him.

"I'll take you shopping later on today if you'd like," Rainer offered.

He didn't like the idea of being parted.

"Perhaps I could order online, and you could go and pick it up?" Keeta suggested. She glanced to see him nod.

"That would be acceptable." He walked over and placed an arm around her shoulders. Sharing time was over.

"Why don't I show you to your room?" Lavina asked.

"Please." Crewe clung to his upbringing. Polite, aloof, and observant without appearing so had served him well.

"How will we be protected from sunlight?" Crewe asked.

"The windows are tinted, painted with a special UV blocking paint, and covered with shutters. We wanted it to be safe, but accessible if necessary," Lavina explained as she guided them up the massive showpiece staircase. "Is she sunlight sensitive?"

"No, she isn't," Keeta answered at the top of the landing. "I can't help but feel like I'm in *Gone with the Wind.*"

"I had the same response when I found it and walked the property for the first time. Though it was a lot less appealing then." She grimaced. "Restoring it was a massive undertaking. There were periods where we all wanted to throw in the towel. In the end, it was worth it. We have a home custom fitted to us. Not many people have that luxury, and the southern do so love their grand manors."

She gestured to the walls painted slate gray. "There were parts we did remain historically accurate, but inside of each room, you'll find modern amenities. Each one has an adjoining bathroom, so you'll have as much privacy as you'd like. There's a computer and a television inside as well. We have cable of course. Roughing it, didn't appeal much." She wrinkled her nose.

They stopped at a thick wooden door at the end of the hall.

"If you need anything, we'll be around. There's plenty of food in the fridge if you're hungry, Nakeeta. There's also a heavily stocked blood fridge in a storage closet."

"You've thought of everything." Who were these people? Their operation ran like a tight ship.

"As much as I'd like to take credit for being clever, it came together over years of planning. Trial and error can be the best teacher. I'll leave you two to settle in."

She sped away, and Crewe opened the door. The light gray walls were adorned with tasteful landscapes that captured Georgia in the four seasons. A master king-sized bed with a pillowed backboard was decorated in white bedding and piled high with pillows.

"I've died and gone to heaven." Keeta ran forward, diving into the center.

Closing the door behind him, he shook his head. A large desk sat in the corner by the blacked-out window, and a flat-screen television rested against the wall next to the door. An antique dresser was placed next to a vanity. The high ceilings and light colors made up for the lack of natural light. Lights set into the wall were aimed around the room and controlled by a dimmer switch. He put them on high as he examined the room.

"You should've been a cop."

"I'm assuring your protection."

"Use your new senses. There's nothing to worry about here."

Sighing, he turned to face her. "I'm not sure how."

"Close your eyes. Center yourself. Let all the worries slip away."

"I can't."

"Crewe. If you don't control this, it'll become a distraction. You know I'm right. It might make you uncomfortable at first, but you know I'm right."

He sighed. "Fine." Closing his eyes, he reached toward the newly developed energy inside of him.

"The energy is a new part of you, not your enemy. Make friends with it."

"What?" A jolt made him jerk. "Ow."

"It'll make your life a living hell as long as you're at odds. All us witchy kids experience it."

"Are you telling me I'm going through puberty?" he asked dryly.

She giggled. "Yeah, I guess I am."

"You speak as if it's a living thing."

"Isn't all energy in some way? Think of it as you do the beast. I know what it's like to live with that now. This is no different; only mine is less aggressive."

Clearing his throat, he focused on the swirling colors of silver attached to the center of his being. It felt odd. Warm when he was used to a cold burn. Acquainting himself with the feel and effects, he relaxed. His beast bristled, before deciding to play nice. It was an odd, alive sensation he'd long forgotten.

"Now reach out with your senses. Feel the magic in the room."

He immediately recognized Keeta's signature. Moving past her, he felt the nuances of other magic settled into the very foundation of the building, around the windows, and the surrounding acres. He perceived no threat or deceit. Pulling out, he rubbed his face.

"Well?"

"All is at it should be."

She nodded her head. "Nicely done, Crewe Gresham."

Her praise warmed him. Speeding to her side, he snatched the book from her hands. "Order clothes. Then we'll eat and rest."

"You still don't trust me alone with them?"

"No."

She knelt on the bed. "Crewe, you can't wrap me up in bubble wrap like delicate china."

"I know." He held her gaze, refusing to back down. "Pick out the clothes, and I'll bring you food."

Placing her hands on her hips, she pursed her full lips. "Are you bribing me?"

"I simply compromising. That's what modern women like, isn't it?" He reached into his back pocket, pulled out the wallet, and slipped his black credit card out. Waving it back and forth, he watched her eyes follow it like a pendulum.

"You're lucky I like you." She snatched the card, and he hid his smirk. She could be a vicious little thing if provoked. It kept things interesting. He could never stand a weak-willed mate. He needed a challenge and someone who could bite back. Soft had never been a word allowed in his vocabulary. While he might cherish her, he couldn't change who he was. She understood that.

"I know," he answered honestly. He watched her move to the computer, reassuring himself that all was well. They'd escaped the others by the skin of their teeth. He wouldn't stop his vigilance now. If you had told him his life would one day revolve around the well-being of a witch, he would have scoffed. Now? She was the heartbeat his undead body could no longer produce.

# Chapter Ten

### KEETA

SHE STARED LONGINGLY AT CREWE'S rippling muscles while he sparred with Cyprian. The purity rituals were putting a strain on her love life. You go three years with zilch, and once you break the seal, you're hooked.

"Pretty to look at, aren't they?"

She grinned at Rainer and nodded. Clad in a light blue maxi dress with pink flamingos, she was much more at home.

"I don't mind that all of our boys are eye candy, but thinking of them in a romantic sense gives me the willies. They're firmly in the family zone, I'm afraid."

Keeta laughed. "I can't help but feel I'm sorry is the only proper response to that."

"Have you found more?" Rainer gestured toward the book she thumbed through with her head.

"Nothing helpful. It's a bit like trying to piece together a puzzle. I get bits and pieces, thoughts that are often scattered." She shook her head. "I'm not sure what she was thinking."

"Seers tend to go insane after a while you know. Too much knowledge of the past, present, and future can become confusing."

Keeta frowned at the bubbly pixie. "You sound as if you speak from experience."

"My mother and grandmother spent their twilight years institutionalized. I fear I'll follow the same trend."

"But you were right about everything."

"And yet, it still takes a toll." Rainer tapped her temple. "Here."

"Can't anything be done?"

"Perhaps if I'm lucky, I will meet my match. The connection can be grounding. The odds, however, of meeting a twin flame in any lifetime are slim."

"You can't see—"

"For myself?" She smiled sadly. "No, that's not how it works."

"It should." The thought of this vibrant woman fading in any way angered her.

"I think if we saw everything coming our way, we'd be insane a hell of a lot faster. There's a reason why they say we have no clue how strong we are until it's our only option."

The book in her hand pulsed. She glanced from it to the woman seated in front of her enjoying the butterflies that danced among the lingering wildflowers.

"Rainer?"

"Hmmm." She turned toward her with a dreamy expression.

"Hold out your hand, please."

"Why?" Rainer eyed her curiously.

"I'm not sure. Just a feeling."

"Okay?" Rainer held out her palm.

The minute the book touched her hand it hummed happily.

"You're one of us."

"What? I don't understand." Rainer shook her head from side to side.

"You're one of the bloodlines, Rainer. Don't you see? That's why you were given this task. How long have you been dreaming about the book and the people here?"

"Since I was young," Rainer said softly.

"What's happened?" Crewe asked.

Cyprian knelt beside Rainer, taking one of her hands between his. "Are you okay?" he asked.

Rainer nodded, her amber eyes still glazed.

"Rainer's had a shock. The book recognized her," Keeta explained.

"Will that *help* her?" Cyprian inquired. For a second, she saw beneath his cool veneer. He truly cared about Rainer.

"Honestly, I don't know. But if I have anything to say about it, it will." She wouldn't give him false hope.

"Your word, witch?" Cyprian said.

"You have it."

"What does this mean?" Crewe asked.

"We're one step closer to recasting our spell." Keeta smiled. Things were beginning to look up.

"And exactly where you need to be," Rainer said with a serene smile. Her eyes went unfocused. "It'll be close."

"What will be?" Cyprian concentrated intensely on her words.

"What's going on?" Keeta went stiff. The timbre of Rainer's voice changed.

"The spell. Not sure if you'll make it."

"Rain." Cyprian cupped her face. "Tell us what you see."

"Could be disaster. Or perhaps, victory? You'll have to work fast and be sure. It'll take a lot of power. They're coming for you. Takes an evil purpose to gather the likes of those forces."

"Tell us about the forces coming, Rain," Cyprian's voice softened.

"Wolves and witches. Vampires, too. Out for blood. They know what you are. Both of you."

"Both of us?" Keeta repeated.

"They won't forget what you did that day. The traitor wants you dead. The vampire. He hates, hates, hates all that's coming. He wants to see it all burn. Been too long on this earth."

"So, *he* wants to take us all with him then?" Crewe narrowed his gaze. "Do you know who this is, Rainer?"

"It's—" Her mouth opened in a soundless scream and her back arched.

"What's happening?" Cyprian cried, holding her against his chest to keep her from harming herself.

"Someone's blocking her." Keeta threw a shield over her friend, and the convulsions stopped. "Be at peace, sister." Rainer slumped in Cyprian's arms. "She's only asleep. When she wakes up, she'll be fine."

Adjusting her in his arms, Cyprian carried her toward the house.

*"Am I the only one who wonders how much Cyprian cares about our little Rainer?"*

*"Caring doesn't make them a love match. Much like wolves, we grow attached to those we consider to be family."*

*"Hmmm."* Unconvinced, she kept her thoughts to herself.

Gripping her hips, he pulled her frame to his. "Does this purity ritual prevent us from kissing?"

"No." His rakish grin was the last thing she saw before his face filled her vision and his lips touched hers. He tasted of berries and desperation. Every day pushed them closer to the ceremony and the uncertainty that would follow. Tilting her head, she deepened the kiss, losing herself in the bond they'd forged, and the love found. If the world burned down around them, at least she had known the beauty of being loved and accepted for everything she was and in spite of what she wasn't.

Crewe pulled back slightly to allow her to breathe as he pressed kisses down her face and neck. His fangs nicked her collarbone, and she quivered.

"Silly witch. Don't you know by now you're everything?" His words threatened to turn her into a puddle.

"Crewe," she whimpered.

"You are the one thing I've done in this life that I'm truly proud of. I'd experience every loss all over again to end up here by your side. Never doubt that."

Burying her face in his neck, she inhaled his aroma and begged her ancestors to keep her safe. *You put us in this position, and you owe me.* She sent the demand out into the universe, knowing he'd somehow hear it.

❈ ❈

"ARE YOU READY?" CIAN ASKED as they waded into the cool water.

Her teeth chattered. "As I'll ever be." The witches gathered at the river to symbolically wash away the negative residue in a naturally flowing body of water, beneath the moon. The vampires lined the perimeter of the area as a precautionary measure. The frigid water quickly spread up her white gown as they formed a small circle. A bracelet and headband made of copper and opals adorned them. Bundles of white sage burned in the small campfire they'd set in the center of stones nearby. The sweet smell coasted toward her on the wind.

Reagan reached down and filled his cupped hands with water. He let the liquid spill, joining the larger source. "With this, we clear way our negative emotion, invite in calm, and heighten our psychic awareness. Like the nature of water, we will be cool, calm, and level-headed."

Closing her eyes, Keeta focused on shutting out the worries, doubts, and painful experiences. Magic worked best when the witch casting was grounded and self-assured. The water lapped against her body, taking away the stress and connecting her to nature. Clear-headed for the first time in weeks, she viewed the star-studded sky with a fresh set of eyes, and experienced the deep communion she'd missed with her surroundings.

Keeta glanced over at the others, and they exchanged gentle smiles. Rainer spoke next. Waving her hands, she brought the smoke toward them with her magic. Circling their bodies, like a cat looking to be petted, it filled her lungs. "Keep our minds clear, and our senses alert." We contemplated the nature of air as the swirls danced before they floated away carried on the wind. Keeta reached into the soft leather pouch around her neck, pulled out sea salt, and sprinkled it into the river. Thinking of the river bed beneath her feet, she connected to the earth, letting the potent force flow through the others in the small circle. "Give us the strength to do what needs to be done. Grant us stability to stand against those who seek to upset the balance."

She experienced complete acceptance. Inhaling sharply, she closed her eyes. A tickling sensation traveled up her arms. Owls hooted a chorus. Crickets serenaded them with their songs. A shooting star blazed against the inky sky as it passed directly overhead. Joining hands, they used the energy they generated to strengthen the fire to a roaring blaze. Intently gazing into the dancing red, yellow, and blue element, she thought on the act of transformation, and how flames could burn away the old to produce something new and pure. The flames twisted themselves into spirals, cracking loudly. They lifted their hands, and the campfire exploded upward, forming a fiery dove.

"I'd say the message was received and rewarded," Reagan drawled.

"Let's close the circle," Keeta said quietly. It felt wrong to break the tranquility that had settled over the land and inside of her mind. The forest had gone soundless, but it didn't feel oppressive. Raising her hand, she drew a circle in the air counterclockwise, as she released the energy they'd gathered. The water rose up, bubbling before it went placid. The silent casting was a new experience. She'd never experienced a circle casually yet sincerely drawn. They gave thanks in their own way, guiding each other with broad directions. She'd always thought of covens as restrictive. These three proved her wrong.

She stepped onto the shore. Twigs snapped to her left, and her ears twitched. Turning her head, she spotted an animal clearing the bushes. The small, brownish-gray coyote and the gray wolf beside him made her gulp. Unafraid, they padded out into a patch of moonlight. Heads held high, they studied her.

"You see this, too, right?" She quickly glanced at Cian who nodded.

"What does it mean?" Rainer asked quizzically.

"In Native American culture, the coyote is a favored form of one of the creators. He represents the spirits of an ancestor. The wolf is a blessing and a way they often choose to communicate with the people." Awed by the physical symbols seeking her out, Keeta bowed to the animals watching her with unblinking eyes.

"Thank you." Her mind traveled to the shaman who'd gone astray. *Now's your chance. They're listening. Don't squander the opportunity.*

The animals appeared to return the gesture before they slunk back into the forest they'd materialized out of like ghosts.

"Are all of your circles this eventful?" Keeta asked with a laugh.

"Ha. Hardly," Cian chuckled.

"Are we ready?" Cyprian asked. Crewe, Silver, and Lavina appeared beside them with blankets in hand.

"Very." Reagan took the blanket from Silver and wrapped it around his shoulders.

"Did everything go as planned?" Crewe covered her with a thick wool cover and pulled her to his side.

"Better than." She smiled, to put him at ease.

"Good." He kissed her temple.

"Here. This should help." Cyprian began to pour tea from a thermos into plastic cups. The blueberry tea warmed them from the inside out, aiding in the further cleansing of their auras. Time was slipping through their fingers like sand through an hourglass and every second counted as the hand of time continued to turn. Truly relaxed, her muscles shed their tension, and exhaustion crept over her swiftly.

"Tired?" Crewe asked as they approached the house.

"Mmm-hmm. Suddenly, I can't even keep my eyes open." She rubbed her eyelids and blinked repeatedly like a small child fighting sleep.

"Here." He seized the empty cup from her hands and unwound the wet blanket from her body on the front porch. "Go ahead and get to sleep. I'll handle this."

"Are you sure?"

"This is my day, remember?" he said, amused.

She hesitated briefly. He'd found a new kinship with Silver and Cyprian. After all he'd lost, she wouldn't begrudge him time to reconnect with people who could understand him.

"All right. Enjoy your dayving." She combined the words day and evening with a wink, adding more cheer than she felt into her words. Wiggling her fingers, she continued into the house, trudging up the stairs.

Inside their room, she pitched her wet things into the hamper and climbed into the shower. Using the rainfall showerhead to the fullest, she chased away the persistent chill. After drying off, she pulled on a pair of pajama pants and a T-shirt, and tumbled face first into the downy paradise of the bed.

Opening her eyes, she found herself in a familiar hollow surrounded by stone. As she sat up on the cold soil, she spotted the Shaman on the opposite side of the fire in the center of the cavern watching her.

Squinting, she observed him silently for a long moment. "Who are you?"

"A person time forgot."

"How can you be remembered when you choose to hide?"

He narrowed his black gaze her way. Sitting up straight, she refused to be intimidated.

"You lay your problems at my feet, and yet you can't share your name with me?"

His nostrils flared. "Seke."

*Seke.* She let the name roll over in her mind. It meant black. *Fitting.*

"It's time you help fix what you broke, Seke."

He sprang to his feet and paced in front of the fire, casting his shadow on the cave wall. "I am not allowed."

"To do what?" She wrinkled her nose, baffled. If he could reach across time to bring her here, why did he act as if he were powerless?

"Anything more than the spirits will allow. This helpless nothingness," he spread his arms wide, "is the state I'm forced to live in."

The petulant tone hit a sour note. "Did you even apologize?"

He scowled. "The spirits care little for regrets."

"Because you've tried? Are you even repentant?" She crossed her arms.

His dark eyes flashed. "You sit in judgment?"

"No. I speak the truth." She rose. "I want to help."

"Help? There is none of that for the damned."

"Stop feeling sorry for yourself and do something," she yelled back, un-ruffled by his dark rage. "While you're here having a pity party, we are risking our lives to stop the very thing you set into motion with your selfish greed. For once, look beyond yourself."

"I have done that. Do you know what it takes to contact you?" He grabbed her wrists. Pain, madness, and sorrow assault her.

*My God.*

"This is my reality. The sentence I must endure for an eternity. You think me uncaring? To feel is to suffer even more than I do now. It's foolishness."

She tugged her hand free and clutched her throat, unable to speak.

"I have accepted the will of the gods. To ask me to do otherwise is too much."

Torn between sympathy and feeling justice had been served, she watched, paralyzed as he receded back into the pitch-black darkness where her eyes could no longer follow. They could expect nothing from Seke.

## SEKE

HE WATCHED, ASTONISHED AS KEETA stood beside the tree just before dawn. Her black dress brushed the ground as she arranged her things in front of her. Facing the north where the sun would rise, she wrote his name on an index card. Chanting softly in her father's native tongue, she pleaded that he be allowed to find peace. He'd forgotten what kindness and purity felt like.

As the sun began its ascent, painting her awash in pinks and oranges as the deep blue gave way to purple, she placed his name in a mason jar full of water. Shuffling her feet, she danced, offering her cries up to the great spirits. He watched mesmerized as memories of his people rushed to the forefront of his mind.

Once, he'd been content to live a simple life in his village. There was always enough food, water, shelter, and company. They worked together to provide for the entire village. It was hard to remember why that stopped now.

Repulsed by her hopefulness, he turned his back on the scene. They gods cared not for mortals and their petty requests.

### CREWE

HE ROAMED THE HOUSE, ENVYING them their ability to retreat into art. His skin felt alive as the nerves kept him on edge. The full moon was fast approaching. He craved distraction from the round robin playing every possible outcome to the spell in his head. Everywhere he looked a member of the pink house was creating.

He stopped in the doorway where Cyprian stood in front of an easel. "What's going on?" he asked, bewildered.

Cyprian chuckled. "It must seem odd to you. It's art day. We have a few days during the month where we replenish our stock to take into town. It helps to keep up appearances. A home full of artists who don't produce would garner unwanted attention."

"I suppose that's true." Crewe leaned against the door frame.

Cyprian continued his steady brush strokes on the once blank canvas. "You have questions?"

"It's an unusual family. I have a hard time imagining how it was formed."

"You've seen the strange effect Rainer can have. Is it hard to believe she fashioned us?"

"I want to know more about who I'm fighting beside. You two give the impression of being extremely close."

"We found one another first. No," he laughed, "that's unfair to her. *She* found me."

"And you listened without ripping her throat out?" Crewe asked skeptically.

Cyprian sighed. "I wasn't in the mood to eat a perky eighteen-year-old girl, who looked twelve on that dreary day in Oregon." He glanced over his shoulder. "Moreover, she reminded me of my soeur, Mariot. We all have our sensitive spots, no?"

"That we do." He'd been right. There was no romantic link between the two. Simply a strong familial bond. Storing the new information, he began to form a deeper understanding of the vampire. A resemblance to his long passed sister would be plenty of reason for a vampire to give a human a chance to get closer than she should. The mind could play funny tricks.

"Mariot died in a famine. As much as I tried to keep her alive, her constitution proved to be too weak. She'd always been a bit fragile." He stated the words like facts, but Crewe sensed the grief behind them. "I could not save her. There's hope yet for Rainer."

"Why was she traveling alone that young? It's a bit unusual for a human that age, isn't it?" Rainer possessed a vulnerability that needed to be guarded.

"Yes, but Rain had no other choice. You heard the fate of the women in her family. Her father and his new wife felt heavy medication and an institution were the best ways to deal with her. She disagreed. So, she ran. The more she trusted her gift, the better she got on. I think that time shaped her into the woman we know." His stern tone indicated show and tell were over.

"You love Nakeeta?" Cyprian asked bluntly.

"Yes." Denying the obvious would be wasted energy.

"It's a dangerous thing, allowing our emotions to connect with humans. Their life spans are short."

"And yet we both know love is not easily controlled," Crewe countered.

"Oh, oui, mon ami." Furious strokes continued to bring the fall scene on the canvas to life. Brilliant oranges, yellows, and greens highlighted the changing leaves on a large oak tree. They stood together in silence as he soaked up the often-elusive peace they'd managed to create in their home.

Satisfied with his talk, Crewe moved through the house, to gather more information. He needed to know the people he would fight beside.

After the betrayal in England, he was low on trust. Keeta's laughter echoed from a room down the hall. He followed the light-hearted mirth and found her seated beside Lavina. For once, her bitter disposition was gone as she worked the foot on her potter's wheel. The misshaped lump of clay in Keeta's hand must be the cause of amusement.

"Looks like you need to practice," Crewe remarked, alerting the women to his presence.

"Yeah, a lot," Keeta said with a laugh.

"Cyprian told me, it's *art* day?"

Lavina gave a tight smile. "Yes, we don't need the money, but it keeps us uninteresting and under the radar." She shrugged.

"What are you making?" He slipped into the room, noting her sudden rigidity.

"With fall coming, I'm making cauldron bowls and mugs." She rolled her eyes. "It's silly, yet people love them."

"Smart. How do you fit into this family?"

"Crewe!"

Lavina waved Keeta off. "No. He's entitled to inquire on our background."

"Is it me you don't like, or another vampire in your territory?"

She had no problem with the others or Nakeeta for that matter. Her lips pressed into a thin line. "A bit of both."

He simpered. "At least you're honest. How have I offended you?"

"Your regime upsets me. You play like you're nice, but the truth is your people are just as ruthless as the rest."

"My regime? That's a powerful word to use. I'm one man."

"Dregan." The name flew toward him like a poison-dipped arrow.

"What quarrel do you have with my sire?" The words were out before he could think on them.

"Even now, you're chomping at the bit to do his bidding blindly. Perhaps, he's not the man you believed him to be. Hmm?"

The words added another black mark to the man he'd all but worshipped. "What did he do?"

"Slaughtered innocents without batting an eyelash."

"You're going to have to be a bit more specific than that." He'd known the man for eons. Her accusations sounded bogus.

"And yet, I don't see him anywhere near you. Doesn't seem as if you trust him." Her words taunted him.

"You know nothing of what's passed between me and my sire."

"And you're not offering up details." She stopped her wheel and stood, hands coated in clay. "Your *sire* ordered the death of an entire coven of vampires."

"Why? You're leaving out details."

"Because *some* of them dared bend the rules. We were before our time, forging a future between witches and vampires. He caught wind of it and felt threatened." Her voice warbled. "So he sent his reapers."

"I'm not aware of this."

"It's the only reason I can stomach working with you. Maybe your *sire* kept a lot more than this from you. I barely escaped with my life." She shuddered.

"Is this true?" Nakeeta turned toward him, stunned.

"I don't pretend to be bevy to all the dealings my *sire* has," he muttered.

"Why would he do that?" Keeta asked breathlessly.

"The threat. Look at what we've done without trying. This sharing of power would be perceived as highly dangerous. If *anyone* knew that, and they sensed an uprising, it would be squashed immediately, and held up as an example." The thought sickened him now. *Would you have thought this before Keeta?* No, he would've seen the action as self-preservation.

"Who did he send?" Crewe spoke around the knot forming in his throat.

"Niall."

The words hit his chest like a two-ton truck. The vampire hated witches and had a cruel streak a mile long.

"I will never forget the screams that rang through the village as my mother ushered me to freedom. I had a brother. She refused to leave him behind. I never saw either again." Her eyes glowed red with anger. "If I ever come into contact with him, one of us won't be walking away."

"He's not a vampire easily bested," Crewe cautioned.

"I'm a survivor with a grudge. Never underestimate what I'm capable of."

Her voice was an arctic blast.

"He is not Niall, Lavina." Keeta stood between them. "I understand you're angry. But keep in mind, Crewe was not there. We can't afford the animosity. I'm sorry about what happened to your family and your village. It's everything we're fighting to stop. Crewe isn't the enemy."

Lavina blinked. "Of course." She returned to her wheel sedately. "I apologize if I made it seem I believed he was."

The jovial mood he'd interrupted lay in shattered remnants.

"I'll leave you two to your art." He excused himself and left the room. *Has Dregan been working against me the entire time? Did I lead him straight to Keeta?* The thought sickened him. In need of air, he swiftly exited the house and took to the woods. What had he been a part of? *How can I know who to trust?* Mind racing, he stalked the forest. The sound of rabbits in the brush caught his ear, and he let go.

The beast exploded outward, shutting down human thought as he tracked the rapid heartbeat, and footfalls. Snatching the fluffy-tailed brownish animal up, he sank his fangs into its neck. The hot blood flooded his throat, and the beast purred in contentment. He pulled away, lowering the limp body to the ground as he licked his lips clean. Letting go was dangerous. He needed to control his emotions. Shoulders slumped, he closed his eyes and felt a gentle tug deep in his mind. *Kaz?*

The call was fuzzy and muddled, like a radio station out of range. *"Crewe."* His name wavered.

*"Why aren't you asleep?* Crewe asked. It was unheard of for a vampire to be awake when he was gone to ground. It was meant to be their version of hibernation.

*"Get … Come … Get."* The connection snapped like a rubber band pushed beyond its elasticity.

*"Keeta, did you feel him?"* He reached out to through the bond.

*"I did. It was him."* Her response reassured him. *"The question is how?"*

*"We need to speak with Rainer."* Hiding the rabbit, he returned to the house.

GATHERED IN THE PARLOR, HE sat in a large, green velvet armchair with Keeta perched on his lap. Her nearness and scent helped him keep a tight grip on the restless beast inside of him. Knowing his friend—his brother—was in distress and aware of being underground, disturbed him.

"What happened?" Cian asked.

"I heard Kaz, in my head."

A cry of anguish spilled free from Rainer. "No."

"You never told me how Kaz figures into all of this," Crewe pressed them further.

"I dreamt of Kazimir." Rainer sipped her tall glass of sweet tea.

"No offense, love, but I have a hard time believing that would've been enough for him." The man hadn't survived by being gullible.

"No. Not at first." Rainer's fingers tightened around the glass. "When I showed him what I saw, things were different."

"What could you possibly show him?" Crewe squeezed Keeta's hips.

"Memories from his past I couldn't have access to, and the future. When I connect to people, I can glean a bit of their past." Rainer looked over his shoulder, seeing what he couldn't. "Some more than others."

"And how did Kaz respond?" Crewe had a hard time picturing the elder dealing with this pint-sized sprite.

"He came to know the truth." Her words felt evasive.

Crewe frowned. "And how is it Kaz contacted me?"

"A spell. It took all of our energy to keep him awake. Your systems aren't built to resist the call to go to ground when it's needed," Cian said.

"And now. He's … what? In limbo? How is that better?" Crewe's shoulders tensed.

"No." Reagan shook his head. "He should be dreaming."

"Impossible." Crewe scoffed.

"You still use this word after everything?" Silver lifted her eyebrows.

"We cast a spell. I was worried he'd be aware in the darkness. This way, he would dream instead. We allowed him to revisit his favorite memories. It serves a dual purpose. The good thoughts would give him a fighting chance at overcoming the darkness we set loose inside of him." Rainer's voice shook.

"The madness?"

"Yes, it's there for all of you in varying degrees, we just … accelerated it," Cian answered.

"What do we need to bring him back?"

"I don't know if we can," Reagan admitted.

"Not acceptable," Crewe snapped.

Keeta squeezed his arm. "Walk us through the spell."

"You need to know he understood the risks involved. He didn't go into this agreement blindly. He went bravely."

Cyprian's words reinforced Crewe's assumptions. He wasn't going to like this. Temper mounting, he listened as they described manipulating parts of his aura.

"You turned him into a ticking time bomb."

"He was already there," Lavina snarled. "We're all hanging on to the ledge by our fingernails."

"Speak for yourself," Crewe countered.

"Must be nice to have a human shield."

Crewe had Lavina pinned to the wall by her throat before she could blink. "You go too far. All this time you've prayed to find the savior who'll fix your problems, and now you can't stand the fact that she has a vampire mate. Do you hate what you are so much?"

Lavina's lower lip trembled.

"You can't hide behind your hate for what's been done to you. I see the disgust every time you eat." Sneering, he scented her shame. "How long have you been hating the skin you're living in?"

"I didn't ask to be this creature." Lav's voice wavered.

"And you can be of no use to us until you reconcile with yourself." Releasing her, he watched as she slid down the wall. "If you attack Keeta in word or deed, I won't hesitate to retaliate."

A sob broke the silence of the room. Her shoulders shook as the dam inside of her burst.

"She was a witch before," Silver informed him. Her brown eyes were full of pity.

It made sense.

"We're going to search in the book for an answer to Kaz." He twined his fingers with Keeta's and pulled her from the room. The weight of things she wanted to see pressed against him through their bond. Still, she held her tongue, until they entered their room.

Keeta sighed. "Do you think that was necessary?"

"I think it was a long time coming."

"You didn't answer my question."

"If you want me to feel bad for hurting her feelings, I can't. She's not the only one with a fucked-up past, and yet we prevail and move forward. If she's not an asset, she's a liability."

"That's not you talking." She pressed her palms against his chest.

"Then who is it?"

"Your past, Dregan, and all of those pretentious trumped up rules you've lived by for far too long."

He turned away. "We're all creatures of habit. Change is hard and terrifying. Lord knows you and I have experienced more than our share in a short amount of time, but we can't shut down or regress. Did you hear what they did to Kaz?" he asked.

"He agreed to it because he knew, like we do, that this is about much more than ourselves. I don't think Lav was the only one hiding behind anger."

He ground his teeth together. Under his skin, in his heart, and mind, she saw the things he didn't want to.

"I've spent my life dedicated to a man I thought had honor. If he's guilty of betraying us, it will all be a lie. What do I do with all of the wasted time?"

"Make up for it by living a life on your own terms, fully awake and aware to the plights and realities of life." She cupped his face. "My mother often told me there are no mistakes, only lessons. It's not a problem until you repeat the same bad decisions. When you got me away from the battle, you made a conscious decision to be on this side of the war. It's something to be proud of."

How could he tell her it was all for her?

"I might be your catalyst, but I'm not your only reason. You were separated from your humanity. We've got you back online now."

"You think the best of me when I don't deserve it. I think you're blinded by love, witch."

"Prove me right, vampire." She nipped his bottom lip. "We've got a book to look through."

# Chapter Eleven

### Keeta

"Let me make sure I understand this correctly. We're going to cast the spell from the book to locate the map, and then use the energy level we raise to break Kaz free?" Regan asked.

Keeta nodded her head. "I couldn't have explained it better myself."

"You're insane," Cian stated blandly.

"Maybe. Are you up for it?" Keeta asked.

"What's a little more peril on top of everything else?" Cian shrugged.

Laughing, Keeta punched Cian's arm lightly. "I knew I could depend on you."

"Rainer?"

Her eyes took on an unfocused appearance. "Yes, it's the right thing to do."

"What I want to know is *how* you plan to do this." Silver crossed her arms and leaned back in her seat.

"We'll amass a huge amount of energy during this spell. Before we close the circle and release it, we'll use it to call him to us."

"If the call is powerful enough, it could work," Crewe said skeptically.

Keeta rolled here eyes, opting to ignore his pessimism.

Rainer stood. "It's time to call the others."

"We're not the only ones who believe in the movement. We communicate remotely online," Lav explained.

"They haven't been vetted. I don't like the breach in security," Cyprian argued.

"If we don't, it'll be the four of us against who knows how many," Silver said. The willowy woman's voice carried in the parlor. The power behind it shocked Keeta. She rose, a warrior fairy, ready for battle. "The time for playing it safe is over. I've already been in contact with them. They are ready and awaiting our command."

"You had no right," Cyprian exploded. "You could've brought them straight to us."

"They know only that we're in the southern states. I was careful. I'm not an idiot, Cy."

"I told her to." Rainer's voice was so soft, Keeta almost missed it. "I saw it, days before Keeta arrived. What's to come can't be survived without them."

"Tell us what you saw." The demand in Reagan's voice was so unlike him she turned her body to see his face. The normally easy-going façade was ruffled. His cheeks were flushed, and his hazel-colored eyes flashed a deep green.

"You might've been next in line for the coven in your parents' tiny town, but you run nothing here." Cyprian's cool voice doused his anger.

"I realize. I-I'm sorry, Rain."

"What's done is done. Now we move forward." Lav sighed, exhausted. "We have one more day until the ceremony. Let them come."

"You're changing your tune?" Silver leaned back, pursing her lips.

Lavina scowled. "What do you want me to do? Continue to behave like a stubborn child. I know I've lost."

"It's not a game." Silver glowered.

"I know that as well as everyone else here, Silver."

Silver and Lavina's gazes lock. The air in the room grew thin. Lav flashed forward a blur. Silver leapt into the air, turning seamlessly into a bat. Keeta's jaw dropped. "You can shift."

The bat flew over to her and changed. "A little present from my maker." Silver grinned cheekily.

"We cannot afford to fight amongst ourselves," Cyprian growled.

"Perhaps, we could all benefit from a friendly spar?" Crewe suggested.

"I think it's necessary." Cian pushed away from the couch and stood. The others followed, heading for the exit.

"This has yet to be resolved," Reagan said.

Cyprian paused by the front door. "You will contact them, and the chips will fall where they may."

Unsure who to follow, Keeta remained with Rainer, who still looked shaken. Walking across the room, she sat down beside her on the gray couch. "Are you okay?"

"I'm afraid."

"That's okay." Keeta took her hand. "We all are, sweetie."

"The things I see are a nightmare played out on the back of my lids, and it all shifts so fast, I've no way of knowing which is the truth."

"The future isn't set. Trying to be the keeper of multiple varied outcomes is madness."

"That's my role. It's my job. My skill is what I bring to the table in this family. If I don't have that …" Rainer trembled like a petrified bunny.

"Rainer. You're the glue that binds everyone together. You're the heart. A vital organ the body can't live without. Don't let the shadows sell you lies."

"The shadows?" Rainer's eyes widened.

"The darkest pieces of us that lead to doubt, loathing, and self-flagellation. Their sole purpose is to deceive. So, we can never trust a word they speak. You're more than your ability to know the future. When we got here, you were the first welcoming face I'd seen it what felt like ages. You treated Crewe and I like old friends, and eased the path between all of us without even trying. It takes a talented person to do that with us temperamental supernatural beings."

She nodded her head, and Keeta felt a kernel of worry began to sprout. Had she gotten worse since they'd arrived? *Move, help her stabilize higher up on the to-do list.*

"You can't save everyone, you know?"

"What?" Keeta blinked. *Did I just hear her correctly?*

"It's important that you realize that. You can't save everyone."

"Why did you just tell me that?" Fear settled in, tightening her chest, and making it harder to breathe.

"I don't know." Rainer shook her head. "I never do." Her tone smacked of agony that made Keeta want to weep.

Smoothing down the skirt of her white sundress with bright yellow sunflowers, Rainer stood. "I need to go send out the messages. I'll see you out there."

Keeta watched the girl go. With one foot in the present and another elsewhere, she was a strange mix of fascinating and sad. *Did she just warn me about future casualties?* Chilled, she made her way outside. The temperature had plunged further, and the sky was overcast and gloomy. As if Mother Nature knew what would soon come to pass.

Pulling her gray cardigan closer to her body, she observed the vampires. Cyprian uprooted a tree without breaking a sweat and flung it at Silver who turned into a black crow and easily dodged the missile. Her jaw dropped. Even for a vampire, that was incredibly strong.

*"It is."* She smirked. Crewe's mind was never far from her own. *"Strength is his talent. I don't need to tell you what Silver's is. Shifting is rare."* Crewe dodged Lavina easily. *"She's fast. But her anger guides her instead of her brain. When she learns to control that, she'll be truly dangerous."*

A flash of bright purple drew her attention to where Reagan unleashed a blast of power toward Cian, who spun and disappeared. Keeta took a step down the front porch, narrowing her gaze as she swept the area. Reagan grunted.

"Potshot, Cian." Reaching out, Reagan grabbed the air. Cian appeared in his hold, grabbed his wrist, and dug his fingers into the nerves. Reagan cried out, releasing Cian's arm, and a powerful blast of energy that clipped Cian before he could move out of the way. Stumbling to the side, Cian laughed.

"That's more like it." He charged Reagan. A clap of thunder made her jerk. She glanced up at the clouds moving across the sky. A flying object caught her gaze. Cian flipped, landing on all fours.

"Show off," Reagan called.

Cian winked. "Years of practice."

"Well come at me, old man. I'll show you how the kids do it these days." Reagan wiggled his fingers.

"If you insist." Cian embodied anarchy as he charged forward, mohawk waving like wheat in the wind, and a wicked grin slashed across his face. The ripped black jeans and Rancid shirt worn with suspenders completed the picture. Black combat boots pounded into the grass.

Reagan threw a bolt of energy. It rebounded off a barrier, and Cian laughed. "Always so predictable." Cian jerked as his body came to a stop.

"Or not," Reagan smirked.

"Well done," Cian remarked, congratulating his cunning.

"I learned from the best." Reagan waved his hand, releasing Cian.

Her hands itched to hold a sword. There was no way in hell she'd stand on the sidelines while they fought her battle for her.

"I think Keeta is growing restless. I'll spar with you, love."

*"When I think I couldn't love you anymore, you go and prove me wrong."* She jogged down the stairs, proud to have a mate who understood she needed to be actively involved.

They answered Rainer's call, coming in waves and clusters. Their magic encroached on the strong wards and spells woven into the property, surrounding areas, and Savannah itself. Her skin itched. Shifting her weight from one foot to the other, she sought out solace on the front porch of the property. With the arrival of the Harmony Coven and the Coven of Night Shadows, the grand house seemed to be shrinking. Trailing her hand over the railing, she let the natural element absorb the excess energy and ground her.

She took a seat in the large, white rocking chair positioned in the corner. Pushing off with her feet, she enjoyed the temporary peace. It all came down to tomorrow. They'd cast the spell under the full moon, and if Rainer's behavior was a predictor, all hell would break loose. The seer had been distracted, absent-minded, and fearful. The concerned looks hadn't gone unnoticed.

"It's the quiet before the storm."

The soft, slightly-accented voice brought her gaze to the petite, olive-skinned vampire from the Harmony Coven.

"Yes," Keeta said.

"You feel the wards being broken strongly?" She tilted her dark head. Keeta hummed her agreement. They'd googled her like she was a Sasquatch who'd left the forest and came to have an intelligent conversation. It was disconcerting. The attention, kneeling, and questions she couldn't truly answer. Like them, she was learning as she went.

She gestured toward the land. "Once you've become attuned to them, you notice the difference when they're agitated. The new energy pouring in is a lot to introduce to a small area at once."

Isadora leaned back, resting her elbows on the rail as she got comfortable. "Yes. We were impressed with the subtle nature of such powerful magic. It takes skill to weave it so seamlessly."

Keeta smiled. "They follow the 'hide in plain sight' method."

"It appears to be working for them."

*"Are you okay?"* Crewe asked.

*"I'm fine."*

Isadora inhaled. "You speak to him in your head? Like we do?"

Keeta blinked, shocked. Isadora chuckled." I apologize. I have a talent for sensing these things."

"Yes. Tell me more about the Harmony Coven," She steered the conversation away from herself.

"We began as a collection of vampires who didn't subscribe to what we've been taught. When you're alive long enough, you learn things are never black and white. When it came to witches and vampires, things were growing increasingly gray. The less effect the sun has, the more we appear to lose our grip on reality. It became all too common to find another old one had succumbed to the madness. The logical answer was to find a witch and ask questions. It took time to *cultivate* a relationship with the right kind of magic workers, but once we did the note comparing began, and we bonded over our common interest and joined into a single coven."

Rocking back and forth, she digested the information. "That's incredible. How long have you been together?"

She wrinkled her brow. "About … five years. We'd heard rumors about the spell and a mother. We always wanted to believe, but there was no sign of real proof or progress. Still, we kept our feelers out there, and made connections with like-minded people also hunting for an answer before the world went to hell." She continued to lean against the railing, facing her. "I think we all know this is our last chance to make things right before it all comes down around us. Our ignorance and fighting amongst one another has led us here. We'll have to work together in order to fix it."

She picked Isadora's brain. "You realize there are others who don't agree."

"Has that ever been a reason for bigotry and hatred to remain?"

Keeta smiled. "No. No, it hasn't." Welcoming the reminder of why they were gathering, she sent the Italian born Isadora a grateful smile. They had to get this right.

Dreary, wet, and cold. Keeta hoped the conditions weren't a sign of how the night would play out. Bundled in a raincoat, jeans, a long-sleeved black T-shirt, and matching boots, she followed behind Crewe, hitching her backpack higher. Stepping carefully, she focused on the upcoming spells as they hiked deeper into the woods. The Covens of Light, Elder Flames, and Liberty had trickled in, upping their numbers to nearly fifty able bodies. Names and faces blurred together as they introduced themselves.

They would act as conduits for energy and the first line of defense. If she had the time, she would marvel at the rare vision of witches working with vampires. It gave them a glimpse of how life could be if they succeeded. Encouraged, she ignored the pins and needles running through her cold limbs. The oppressive feel of impending disaster weighed down on her shoulders. Lightning streaked across the sky followed by a loud boom of thunder. Wind howled. Reminded of the night their wards were breached in England, she quickened her pace.

"We need to hurry. The others aren't far behind," Rainer stated.

"How close?" Crewe asked.

"Hard to say."

"We should run then," Cyprian said.

"Ready?" Crewe grabbed her around the waist.

Nodding, she buried her face in his neck as he pushed off from the ground. The wind brushed against her fast. A fine mist of light rain coated her eyelashes and exposed face. Her heart galloped in her chest like a wild stallion eager to run free. She'd never get used to traveling like this. What would've taken an hour was covered in minutes. They landed in the clearing gently.

She nuzzled his neck. "You're getting better at this."

He grinned. "Practice makes perfect and all that."

She memorized the feel of their bodies pressed together before stepping back. The moon imbued her with its power, leaving her feeling floaty like she'd downed too much allergy medicine. She turned to the others, ignoring the icy rain that ran down her neck.

"Let's stick to the plan, form our circles, and get a cauldron set up over a fire." They were going old school for this spell. Every detail would be followed with careful attention to detail. The vampires spread out, taking strategic positions around the area while the witches began to prep. Crewe would be the last line of defense; remaining just outside of the final circle she would cast. His nearness reassured her. Steadying her shaking hands, she watched as Cian and Reagan quickly erected a covering.

"Anin, Ursa, if you'd be so kind as to help us light a fire." The stocky, dark-haired Scot and his petite, dirty-blonde haired coven mate hurried over. Ursa lifted her hand, using her deep connection with water, to dry out the area in the fire pit marked by a ring of stones they took pains to etch powerful runes on. Keeta watched amazed as the water receded back into the ground.

The wood kindling went from a dark brown wet mess to a dried out light brown with white marks.

"Amazing." Keeta smiled.

"Aye." Anin held up his hand. A spark shot free onto the wood scraps, and the fire crackled to life. Crouching, Anin continued to coax the fire to grow while they lifted the cauldron onto the metal tripod. Drying the pot out with a thought, she stood to her full height.

"Once we properly draw the protective circles, we won't be able to see or hear what goes on beyond. I'll give everyone a few minutes."

Crewe turned and stepped beneath the covering. Winding her arms around his neck, she dove forward, tasting his lips. Their tongues slid together as she sampled his flavor. The succulent taste of his blood coated her mouth. He'd nicked himself with his fangs. Leveling up like Mario after he ate a mushroom in Super Mario Brothers, she moaned as his power raced through her veins. He'd fed well. His love filled her, chasing away the fear of failure and self-doubt. Panting as they parted, she rested her forehead against his.

"Upon my last breath, I swear I will allow nothing to harm you."

She took a deep breath and forced herself to let him go. Her heart wept as they stepped apart.

"Let's cast the circle." Storing her emotions away, she removed her raincoat, and shimmied out of her pack, placing it beside the fire. Unzipping the main compartment, she started to remove the orgonite pyramids. The resin structures had been handmade with a variety of things. The silver, white, and gold piece she held in her hand was crafted with fluorite, amethyst, and onyx, specifically for protection. Kneeling, she rested it on the edge of the perimeter and moved on to the next one.

With the circle clearly defined, she admired her work. Firelight flickered off the colorful pyramids. Reaching into the backpack, she pulled out the blessed sea salt. Rolling the chunky pieces between her fingers, she reinforced the circle with a physical layer. A low-level hum began as the energy of the twenty people gathered in the space and began to build. Pleased with her work, she placed her elemental items, a clay pot crafted by Lav for earth, a copper bell for air, an ornate jade dragon for fire, and a large conch shell for water.

Next, she removed her wand. The crystal quartz with black tourmaline and moonstone served as the perfect way to focus her energy. The bits of turquoise, onyx, and copper used to help decorate all worked together. It felt like she was holding a lightning rod. Standing straight, she began to cast the protection. Facing north, she held the wand up, envisioning a white thread as she moved to the east, connecting each point she drew out

Facing east, she picked up the bell and rang it. "We honor and welcome the transitional winds." The wind ruffled the thick hair she'd pulled back into a braid. Goosebumps rose on her flesh. "We call you and ask you to make our steps light as a feather and our voices powerful shouts of conviction and intent." The bell swung back and forth, echoing into the night. Resting it back into its place, she moved clockwise to the south, carefully extending the vision of the white ribbon in her mind's eye with her wand aiming true.

Picking up the jade dragon, she ran her fingers over its smooth surface as she imagined the heat of fire, flowing through her body. "We honor and welcome the burning flame. We call and ask you to ignite the spark of life and energy behind our eyes. Enable us to destroy and create with white-hot power." The fire jumped high, rising far above the cauldron before it shrank back down. The others gasped at the physical manifestation of her will. Returning the figure to its place of honor, she slowly turned clockwise to face west.

The shell was smooth in her hand. Honing in on the falling rain, and the smell of the sea salt, she imagined the waves crashing into the shore. "We honor and welcome the tides. We call you and ask you wash away the doubts that cloud our minds and grant us motion and purpose. Our emotions are as powerful as our bodies."

Resting the shell onto the ground, she began her final rotation back north. Holding the clay pot in her hand, she felt the energy of the makeshift family who'd adopted her into their ranks as it rose up to comfort her and keep her shaking hand steady. She imagined them as an unmovable rock. A powerful, natural structure tested and weathered by the elements, but never destroyed. "We honor the earth. We call upon you and ask you to remind us of our strength and how far we've come. Just as you endure, let us grow and meet every obstacle that comes our way."

She walked to the center of the circle in front of the fire, picturing the white ribbon growing brighter.

"Oh, God. I see it," Rainer whispered. The translucent white stripe shimmered, iridescent and breathtaking. The powers that be were here and listening. Glancing at everyone in the circle, she envisioned their bodies filling with the powers of the elements.

"With fire in our heart, air in our lungs, water in our veins, and earth beneath our toes, we come. Let this space strip us of all our pretenses and connect us with our deepest hidden parts and the world around us. We give thanks to the elements that stand guard against our enemies, the energies that thrum at our fingertips ready to be wielded, and the forces our eyes have been opened to." Her hands rose into the air. "We dedicate this space to be the base where we project our power and intent. Lend us your protection." She cried her request. The words seemed to echo in the night, bouncing around them.

"Goddess," someone whispered as a wind tore through the circle, winding around their waists, tugging at their clothing and hair before it moved out of the circle. Her lips parted as a twisting wall of a whirling tornado obscured them from view. The scent of the beach wafted through the circle. Rain pounded the ground, forming a circle of water. The elements were forming walls between them and danger. Her gut clenched. A flame of fire sprang from the ground, burning bright and hot. She could smell the ash and smoke. The ground rumbled beneath their feet, cracking. A chasm formed around them.

"T-the circle is c-cast," Keeta stuttered.

"I have never seen a circle so powerful," Cian said.

"We've been feeding this ground our energy and blood in preparation. It makes sense," Rainer added.

"Not just our blood," Keeta reminded them. *Is this what happens when vampires and witches combine their will?* "Now we start our spell." Keeta removed the vials of blood from the black backpack.

### CREWE

"Mein got." The partitions of whirling winds, water, and fire sent un-adulterated panic racing through his body. He started toward the barrier and paused. Amazement and excitement flowed freely through their bond.

"They're okay. Continue raising the wards," Crewe called. There were thirty of them positioned strategically. A mixture of witches and vampires, working as one to keep the world from going to hell. It sounded like a teen sitcom. Yet, here they were. He felt the magic come up from the ground. Their blood soaked the grassy floor.

The addition of the newcomers kept them bound to the cause and strengthened the spells. They wanted their enemies as depleted as possible, and those fighting beside them to be bonded by more than their word.

Lightning streaked the sky. The color triggered memories.

"Shit."

"What?" Cyprian asked.

"We're about to experience a gift that keeps giving like the plague. Those wards are about to be tested."

"You know who's coming?"

He snickered. "I have a clue. A Voodoo priestess with a grudge named Genevie."

"What's her quarrel with you?"

"My mate. And I can tell you now, she's going to be swimming in power if she's taking a chance on round two."

"That means she got her ass handed to her last time," Silver said with a laugh.

Grinning, Crewe nodded. "She made the mistake of underestimating Nakeeta." He kept their history to himself. It wasn't his story to tell.

The wind kicked up, and creeping fog begin to trickle in.

"Here we go." *Bang*. Magic battered the barriers they'd set. He cracked his neck and took a fighting stance. The opposing magic felt wrong, like bugs creeping over his skin. Jittery, he glanced around at the others positioned around the area. Lavina stood in the middle beside Silver and Eoin, a Scottish vampire from the Elder Flame Coven.

The burly, brown-haired man had a chest like a barrel and wild locks that framed his square-shaped face. With hands like hammers, it made sense that his specialty was strength. Not far away in staggered lines Merrill, Pauline, and Gunnar, their swift runners stood, ready to catch them unaware.

THE MEMBERS OF THE COVEN of Liberty were a mixed bag. Vampires of various ages from the United States, they stood tall, lithe, and blond. With their dark blue eyes, high cheekbones, and cupid's bow lips, they could've been siblings. Their maker clearly had a type.

Their wards held. Illuminated by lightning strikes, the sky exploded with white hot streaks. Thunder rumbled, resonating through his chest.

"I don't know how much longer it'll hold," Fern cried. Freckles stood out on her pale face as her wild curls were ripped from their braid.

"Ready the first wave," Nair barked in a thick Scottish brogue. The lead witch from the Elder Flame Coven readied his people.

Intense heat lines wavered in front of the barrier. The shield faltered. They saw the group amassed.

"Steady," Crewe called. *Will the people I considered friends be on the opposing side?*

One last bang and the wall melted, like crayons under attack by a blow dryer.

"Now," Nair called. The powerful sleep spell knocked the first row of people off their feet. Bodies hit the ground.

"First you run, and now you attack." Dregan's voice twisted his gut. "What should I expect from you next?" The sight of his men lined up behind his sire gutted him. Disbelief, disappointment, and confusion lined Louis and Pierce's faces. The knife in his chest twisted.

"You come here aggressively attacking us, and yet you question me?" Crewe asked.

"You have my property," Dregan replied. He was in rare form, clad in leather leggings covered in a leather suit, worn and weathered by age and battle. His blond beard had two braids and silver beads. He clutched his sword tightly.

"*She* is not a thing to be owned," Crew replied.

"And yet she decided the future of all people. I can't believe after all of this time you abandon me for a woman." He sneered.

"You betrayed us." Crewe spat onto the ground.

"The traitor has been dealt with." Dregan's blue eyes flashed to red.

"And I've kept Keeta safe."

"Then why are we at opposite ends?" Dregan boomed.

"Because you're a fool," a third voice supplied.

Dregan jerked. A sword pushed out of his chest, and blood ran down the corners of his mouth. "I've had enough of waiting." Niall kicked his body to the ground and lifted his sword, cleaving Dregan's head from his shoulders.

"No," Crewe's scream joined Morena's. Men he'd fought beside rushed forward, slaughtering each other in the pandemonium that broke free. He wanted to rush forward, but his loyalty lie with the woman behind the wall of elements. His eyes watered.

Morena was a ball of red flame, burning everything in her path as she fought to get to Niall. Sparks exploded from Dregan's body as he burned. His past and direction went up in flames with his old leader. Swords clanked together, blood flew, and bodies hit the ground. The fog continued to creep up to waist level.

Morena's fire was extinguished as Genevie crept into view. Sputtering, Morena turned to face the witch.

"I had hoped to settle this like gentleman. But I see now that won't be possible." Niall's voice rang out from somewhere in the center. "So we'll be taking what's owed. We've waited in the shadows long enough. It's our turn to rule. The humans squander their resources like the hairless apes they are. What has begun is evolution."

"It's the result of greed, envy, and hate," Morena barked.

"I'm sad to see you think so, sister." Genevie's voice was thick oil, greasing its way over the senses.

"I am not your sister." A ball of energy exploded, knocking the dark-haired witch off her feet.

"She wants to play." Genevie landed four feet away. "I'm always up for a game." She sent out a dark cloud of energy that turned into black cobras, fangs bared.

Morena cut their heads off with a quick wave of her hand. With the mutiny finished, and the sides chosen, the true battle began. Bloodied and injured, but alive, Louis and Pierce joined him along with a handful of others. Niall had been planning this for a long time. *How long has he twisted his own agenda, in the name of Dregan?* The name made his heart bleed. *I'm sorry I doubted you, old friend. I'll win this in your name.*

"Last chance to choose the winning side," Niall bellowed. Silence reigned. "Show them no mercy."

*Show them the same courtesy they have shown you,* a wicked voice spoke inside of him. Unlike his beast, this was cool and calculating. He embraced the witch. *Yes, let's show them ... for Dregan.* Allowing the instinct to take control, he lifted two witches off their feet. Pinning their arms to their sides, he twisted his hands, snapping their necks. They dropped to the ground, limp and useless. *Let the fire take them like it took Dregan.* Two bolts of lightning struck the bodies, setting them aflame. The smell of burning flesh had never been enjoyable until now.

He met Niall's gaze from across the field. A tiny frame broke their staring contest. He recognized the deep red locks immediately. *Lavina.* Niall's face flew to the left. Nail lines appeared across his cheek. Rage distorted his face into a grotesque mask. He turned toward her to find her gone. Using her speed, she took pot shots, taking her pound of flesh one slice at a time.

Unable to look away, he tracked them. Blood splatter crusted onto his black pants and shirt. Niall moved to give chase. A bolt of power drove into his side. He turned to the left and Silver jumped on to his back, driving her teeth into his neck. He grabbed the back of her neck, and she morphed into a bat, flying away. Niall roared. Dirt exploded a yard way. Morena hit the ground, rolling away from the strike Genevie intended for her. Blood ran down Genevie's face. Her black dress was ripped and muddied. Morena bled from a gaping wound in her side. Her black pants were ripped at the knees. Scorch marks were burned everywhere on her clothing. Her hair stood on end as electricity crackle down her body.

Genevie spun her hands, gathering a ball of shimmering purple energy. Thrusting her hands out, she sent a roaring serpent-shaped blast toward Morena. Facing the energy down with unflinching energy, she stood her ground, chanting softly. At the last possible second a shield shimmered in front of Morena, and the magic returned to its sender. The serpent struck Genevie in the shoulder, sending her to her knees. Morena smirked and moved in for the kill. A petite, mocha-skinned witch jumped in front of her, as a dark-skinned man with glowing hands hid them in a cloud of black smoke.

A strangled cry rang out. Crewe watched as Niall ripped Lav's heart from her chest. Silver screamed and tore at his eyes with her claws. The vampires and witches continued to advance on them.

"Looks like we're almost up." Cyprian strained to remain beside them. He could feel the vampire's deep anguish.

"He will pay, Cyprian. I promise you that."

"It's how she would've wanted to go. Fighting him."

Silver flew away crookedly, wing torn.

*"Whatever you're doing. You need to finish swiftly."*

# Chapter Twelve

### Keeta

An invisible hand reached into her chest and gripped her heart. Gasping for air, she clutched her shirt. A bright white light exploded from the cauldron. Heat coated her. Pulled from her feet, all of her nerves fired at once, and she screamed. Drops of blood left the cauldron, coming together to form a map of countries suspended against air. The final drop joined the display, and a map solidified. The light brown worn leather glowed gold before it floated to her hands.

Her fingers touched the edges, and fireworks went off behind her lids. Locations, latitude, and impressions of people flooded her brain. The map disappeared.

"No." Dumped onto the ground, like a broken doll, she sobbed at the barriers around them wavered. *There's no time. You have to call Kaz.* Gathering what was left of their will and the power they'd called forth, she used Crewe's knowledge of his location and sent the command.

"Rise, Kazimir Anton Koziol." Spent, she rested her head on the grass.

"Why are you sad?" Rainer whispered.

"I lost the map."

Rainer smiled. "No, it's hidden." She held out her hand, and Keeta took it, standing. "It's a place no one can penetrate." Her petite hand landed on Keeta's chest. "Here. Call it forth." Reaching into her chest, she pulled out the leather wrapped into a scroll.

"We've done it," Cian marveled. The others fell to their knees, breathing heavily. Channeling energy was exhausting.

"They're in trouble. I can feel it," Keeta whispered.

Reagan shook his head. "Once we lower that barrier, we'll be sitting ducks like this."

Crewe's distress led her to make an executive decision. "We take the energy amassed and use it for our will. Refuel us, guide us, and allow us to obtain our goal. So we will it so mote it be."

Vibrations shook their way up her body, sloughing off her weariness. Her ancestors wanted to restore the balance. They hadn't left her yet. The fire burned an eerie green, and the smoke rising formed a shape. *Seke?* Clad in his leather breechcloth, buckskin leggings, and wolf pelt he felt as solid as she.

"I will take the brunt of the battle when the barrier is lowered. Your people need help if they're to survive."

"How are you here?" she asked, stunned.

"I was wrong. The spirits listen when you ask for the right reasons." The serene smile he gave her shocked her into silence. "Lower the barrier." His eyes glowed yellow, and his body turned misty as he became the largest wolf she'd ever seen. The brownish-red beast came to her chest.

Turning to the west, she held her hands up.

"Powers of the West of Water we thank you for your presence here today for sharing your deep mysteries and intuition. Hail and farewell." Seaspray caressed her face as the wall of water came down. She continued the farewell to each direction, feeling their acceptance of their thanks before they removed their protection. Heart pounding in her chest, she ended the ritual.

"The circle is open, but never broken."

The shroud that hid them disappeared and they were left looking at their people. Dead bodies from both sides littered the ground. Crewe and Cyprian were locked in battle with vaguely familiar vampires. Witches battled one another. The stench of burnt flesh, blood, and singed grass and dirt turned her stomach. Seke charged forward, sinking his teeth into the vampire holding Silver down.

"Nakeeta."

Harper limped toward her covered in blood. Her hands glowed with purple flames. Her eyes bled black.

"You sold your soul." Sorrow welled in Keeta's chest.

"You helped me with that."

"I may have started you on the path, but you were the one who chose to continue to walk farther." The time for guilt had passed.

"Is that what you tell yourself?" The flames in the palm of her hand grew, flickering wildly.

"That's what I know."

"Then we'll have to reeducate." She shot a fireball at Keeta who jumped out of the way.

"What the hell are you?" Harper spun, tracking her. Fire flew in wild arcs Keeta avoided with large leaps. The cold feel of fingers in her brain made her falter. Distracted, she misjudged and landed wrong. Separated from the control of her bodily functions she peered around, seeking the source of the enchantment.

"Did you actually think you'd bested me?" Genevie slinked in front of her.

"I think someone might've beat me to it." She spoke coolly as she examined the mental ensnarement, untangling it like a ball of yarn.

Genevie grabbed her face, squeezing. "I'm going to enjoy hearing you scream. The only request they have is that you remain alive, not unharmed."

Popping the spell like a lock, she grinned.

"Too bad you'll be disappointing them." Her hand shot up. She grabbed her wrist, and twisted, bringing Genevie to her knees. "I think it's time for you to experience the pain you've given to others."

> *Wolf and horse, old signs of might,*
> *Lend your strength to me this night.*
> *The pain and grief they so easily give,*
> *Must be returned so they can live.*
> *To know and feel what they have done,*
> *And change their ways, with harm to none.*
> *Send back the pain, teach them this night,*
> *And help them to do what they know is right.*

She grabbed both sides of her face as she chanted. Genevie froze. Her eyes dilated, and she began to scream. Releasing her face, she tossed the woman to the ground. Harper stared at her flailing leader with disgust.

"Somnum." She sent the powerful sleep spell to the distracted woman. Dark energy pulsed inside of her, making Keeta wonder if she was in charge or being ridden by a dark spirit. Compelled, she bent, and placing her hand on her forehead she imagined a gold cord linking her to the darkness. Slicing the cord mentally, she considered her debt paid in full. Stepping over her prone form, she sped over to jerk the female vampire off Crewe.

Hefting a blade, he matched Niall stroke for stroke, blocking and thrusting. He landed a blow to his arm, and she mentally cheered. The blonde vampire rushed her, and she ducked, flipping her over her shoulder. The shock on her face was nearly comical. The blonde hissed, and the beast inside answered. Keeta's teeth lengthened, and she snarled. *Show her who's in charge.* The beast had been challenged. She could do nothing more than answer.

Launching herself at the girl, nails elongate, she slashed her chest and waist, ignoring the sting that ran down her arms. She spun to face her again. Nairthan came up beside her and slammed her down over his knee, breaking her back as he ripped out her throat. He spat her flesh onto the ground as she bled out.

"Hate to ruin your fun, lass, but you're too precious to be risked."

"Thank you." He nodded. "Things are getting a bit hairy."

They were losing ground and stamina.

✿ ✿

PUSHING AGAINST EACH OTHER, CREWE and Niall refused to give an inch. Rain pounded down on their heads, turning the ground into a muddy marsh. Shivering she took in the decimation. Clumps of blood, limbs, charred remains, and bodies dead and dying were strewn on the forest floor. The carnage sickened her. How many more times would this scene play out? If Niall had his way, this would be a way of life on Earth. *Never.*

The cool caress of invisible fingertips drew her attention to a light fog rolling in. Seke bounded over to stand beside her, tugging on her arm gently.

"You want me to follow you?"

His head bobbed up and down.

"Okay." He led her to a large oak tree. Power radiating off it stole her breath. The fog came from the opening at the bottom. "The spirits."

Seke's massive head nodded. He gestured toward the tree. Placing her hand on the trunk, she gasped. They were coming. Figures formed in the mist, walking onto the field. Various shapes and sizes, and clothing styles, they gathered, joining hands around the wide perimeter. The ancestors of the bloodlines wronged and her own had enough spilled blood. The pressure built inside of her. Panting, she dug her nails into the bark.

*Let go. We'll handle the rest.* Obeying, she closed her eyes, becoming a conduit for them to deliver their own brand of justice. A loud clap of thunder sounded. The air around them exploded into light. Warm rain pattered onto her wet clothes. A scream rang out. She watched as the first person clutched their head and fell to the ground writhing. They followed, dropping one by one in the grass.

A gaunt figure stepped through the mist. His black hair was a nest of tangles, and dirt clung to the exposed parts of his skin.

"Kazimir?" she whispered.

"The spirits have bought us time. We need to go. She needs us."

"Who?"

"My mate. The final one who'll complete the spell."

Crewe thrust the sword into Niall's throat and spat on his body. She felt the roar of his beast as he avenged his sire.

Rainer appeared beside them. "We have to go."

"Lavina," Silver croaked.

"The time for mourning will come later." Cyprian placed a gentle hand on her shoulder.

The vampire bit her bottom lip and nodded as she sucked back her tears.

"What about this?" Keeta gestured to the ground.

"We'll handle it," Reagan said.

"Go." Silver pushed them away.

"No, all of us. The wolves will come next," Rainer whispered. "None of us can be here when they arrive."

"How far?" Cyprian asked.

Rainer shook her head. "I can't see it."

"We will split up. It'll make it harder to track us," Nair suggested.

"Now," Rainer screamed.

"You know where to meet later?" Cyprian asked as he took Rainer's hand.

"Yes." Crewe nodded.

"In a week's time. We arrive. Godspeed." Cyprian swept Rainer into his arms and took off like a shot.

Kazimir grabbed Crewe's arm. "We must find my mate now. She's in danger. The witches. They showed me things while I was in the ground."

"The map," Keeta whispered.

"Later, my friend. We won't be much help to anyone if we're captured or killed. Can you keep up as you are?"

Kaz nodded. "I've dined well tonight on the blood of my enemies."

"I know we don't know each other well, but that's the kind of creepy shit old vampires need to work on not saying," Keeta mumbled.

His laughter chased her as she wrapped her body around Crewe's before he took into the air.

�֍ ֍

THEY'D WON. YET THE VICTORY felt hollow. Shell-shocked, they showered and changed in a townhouse Kaz kept in Tennessee.

"Did you get the map?" Crewe leaned back against the headboard as she towel-dried her curls.

Sending him the vision through their link, she watched amused as his eyes widened.

"That's one way to keep it safe."

She chuckled. "We should go talk to Kazimir, and see what else he learned."

"In a minute." He sat up on the edge of the bed and tugged her to stand between his legs. "Let me look at you for now."

Sitting on his lap, one knee on either side of his body, she bent to kiss his lips. "We're okay," she whispered.

"For a minute, I was afraid we wouldn't be." The admission shook her.

She nodded. "Me too."

"That was too close."

"We have to find Kaz's mate, and end all of this."

"Soon." He rolled her over and crawled on top of her.

"We don't—" His lips on her neck silenced her response. "Maybe we have a few minutes." Arching her neck, she sighed as his fangs, caressed her pulse point.

A knock sounded on the door.

"I'd say I hate to interrupt, but for those of us who are waiting to find our mate, it'd be a lie."

"Gods' bones." Crewe dropped on his back in the bed. "We'll be there shortly, Kaz."

"Appreciated, brother."

"Let's go. Kaz never lets anything go. He'll come back in a few minutes if we don't join him."

She covered her mouth, trying to hide her laughter.

"Think this is funny, do you?"

"I've never seen you respond to anyone like this."

"Kaz is my elder." Crewe shrugged.

"And you like him. In a way you didn't feel with your sire."

Crewe paused. "A sire bond is something you feel whether you want to or not. What Kaz and I developed was more genuine."

"I get it. Friends are the family we choose for ourselves."

"If I want to keep this *friend,* we'll join him." He set her onto her feet and stood, twining their fingers. They walked out into the living room where he served a warmed mug of what she knew wasn't coffee and a box of pizza.

"I don't keep human food in the house, so I ordered out. I hope that was okay."

"It was perfect and thoughtful. Thank you, Kazimir."

"Please, call me Kaz. You're basically my sister-in-law." He smiled politely. Clean and dressed in black slacks, and a white button-down shirt, he cut an imposing figure as he towered above her five-foot-nine inches. They seated themselves around the cocktail table where the food was laid out. Kaz took the brown leather lazy boy, and they took the couch with the matching décor. The massive fireplace was a centerpiece decorated with interesting art pieces. The walls were a bachelor beige along with the carpet. The furniture consisted of exquisite dark wood antiques.

"Do you know anything about your mate, Kaz?"

"Only her name and her face. Joss."

The map warmed up inside of her chest. "I get the feeling we won't have a hard time finding her, Kaz."

"She kept me sane while I was under. I dreamt of her and spoke with the witches. They want the balance returned." His gaze took on a faraway expression.

"We'll start the search tomorrow, Kaz. Tonight, we rest. I know I need a minute." Her voice wavered. She thought of Lavina, so brave and fearless with her flashing eyes and russet hair, and Morena who'd been unconscious the last time she saw her. *I don't even know how many died.*

Kaz bowed his head. "Of course."

Rainer's warning echoed in her mind. *You can't save everyone.* Suddenly, she understood exactly why seers went insane.

"Eat." Crewe pushed a plate of pizza into her hand. "You need to keep your strength up. I can feel your exhaustion from here."

She forced the triangular wedge of cheese and sauce into her mouth. It tasted like cardboard in her mouth. How could she enjoy anything when so many lives had been snuffed out? Still, it made him and her body happy, so she chewed and swallowed. Tomorrow they'd face the task head-on. She'd be stronger, sharper, and more put together. Tonight, she would focus on finishing her food without breaking down, and wrestle with the guilt that came with being a survivor.

An irritating burn near her heart hit. Plopping down the paper plate, she shifted on the couch. In search of relief, she rubbed her sternum. The feeling increased, spreading.

"Keeta." Crewe's voice sliced through the haze. "What's wrong?"

"I'm not sure." Inhaling, she closed her eyes. A misalignment in her spirit screamed out silently. "Something's wrong. I've never felt this before." A rhythm tapped inside of her chest. She placed her fingers between her breast. The digits sank in, and she cried out. Her fingertips caressed the leather edges of the map. Gripping the rolled item, she pulled it out.

"What is that?" Kaz asked

"The map that will lead us to the others." The map flowed with a golden light. Her hand shook as she unwound the scroll, and the ink moved like a living thing, snaking across the page. Twisting and writhing, the lines appeared agitated. "I don't know what I'm supposed to do," she said. *Blood.*

The voice inside her head made her sit up straight.

"What?"

"Blood." She held up her wrist. "Bite me." Crewe sank his teeth into her wrist, and she let the droplets fall. The red beads rolled together. "Yours too," she whispered.

"Mine?" Crewe asked.

"Yes. I think you were chosen, too. You see things others don't for a reason."

"We're connected," Crewe said.

"Yes, but I believe it may be more than that." She gestured toward the map. "Add your blood."

Breaking the skin on his wrist with his fangs, he added a few dark drops.

Their blood mingled, and crept over the map. Red dots pulsed. The letter R appeared in Massachusetts. *Rainer.*

"Rainer and Cy are safe. They're in Massachusetts." She tapped the point. "Look."

Kaz appeared beside her. "Can you see Joss?"

"No." Her stomach sank.

A crescent moon in blood appeared above Montana.

"Looks like we're heading west."

# *The End*

*The adventure continues in the sequel, Bad Moon*